In the Smoky Air

In the Smoky Air

Alok Joddha Hernández

InnerWorld Publications
San Germán, Puerto Rico
www.innerworldpublications.com

All rights reserved under International and Pan-American Copyright Conventions. Published in the United States by InnerWorld Publications, PO Box 1613, San Germán, Puerto Rico, 00683.

Library of Congress Control Number: 2011929519

Cover Design © Lourdes Sánchez (Mukti)

ISBN: 9781881717126

Prologue

In the mountains, there's a valley. In the valley, there's a town—a college town, or so it's known. It has one main street, and a river that marks its western border. At the southern edge of town is the college, surrounded on all sides by forest and trees. At the end of summer, every year, young students migrate from elsewhere and abroad and descend upon the town, upon the college, and temporarily drink and revel and call the valley their home. They mingle among each other; something about the woods unnerves them. There is one road that cuts through the trees and connects the campus to town, but who takes roads? Dark, winding walkways dissect the forest; they spread out from the campus in living, spidery vines.

At the end of one such path there was a road, an old road, lined on both sides by dilapidated, decaying Victorians designated as off-campus "student housing" by the natives who wanted nothing to do with them. At one end of the road there were the woods; at the other end was town, Main Street being only a quarter mile away. A low, thumping bass pulsed deeply in the darkness; it came out from one house, set back against the trees at the end of the woods. A party was taking place, but almost no one was outside; the summer heat was dense, in spite of the night.

Inside, where it was cool, the students huddled within the house's thin, plaster walls. There was central air conditioning; it remained comfortable no matter how many people came.

But it didn't smell right in there. Half-empty keg cups were strewn on every surface and where there was no surface, the floor sufficed. And it was loud. Pounding sound and shrieking freshmen girls. The whole house reeked like the tail-ass end of a stale beer.

Outside, there were others—two of them. The boy's name was Adam, and the girl's name was Allie. Allie knew the boy's name; but the boy didn't know hers.

The boy appeared to be alone, and perhaps even thought as much, but Allie moved like a cat when she walked; she approached the boy from across the front lawn, and the boy didn't see her until she was just standing close.

"Hey," she said, "aren't you in my mythology class?"

The boy had sweat on his brow from the heat. He held his drink up by his lips, as if in deliberation. "Sure," he said, "I remember you."

Allie's eyes were green and sharp. They narrowed like slits when she spoke to people. She was drunk, was what she said. Was drunk and stoned and barely knew where she was. Could he walk her back to campus, or maybe even back to her dorm? She heard the campus was dangerous for girls to walk around on at night. She heard that people got raped in the woods.

The boy stuffed his free hand in his pant pocket. "I don't know," he said. "My girlfriend's supposed to meet me here later, otherwise maybe I would."

"What's her name?" Allie asked.

"Rachel."

"Rachel?" she asked. "I know Rachel. I saw her dancing at P&G's, and probably with some other guy."

The boy looked at her; Allie was smiling. "I don't know anything about P&G's," he admitted. "This is my first semester."

"You're a freshman?"

"Yeah. I guess I am."

"I know P&G's," she said. "It's where the pop-your-collars dwell."

The boy couldn't help but smile now, too, and Allie approached him closer. "So are you going to give a drunk girl a walk home ... or aren't you?"

The woods leading to campus are not lit by lights. Officially, the college discourages people from walking them, and particularly after sundown. They can't be held accountable, the college often says, and so the dirt pathways remain lit only by moonlight, by starlight; they echo with the din of drunk students, laughing in the fullness of the night.

That night Allie and the boy walked the paths with only the pale glow of the full moon to light their way. The boy led Allie by the elbow, until she grew tired of the setup and accommodated herself further, wrapping her arm around his shoulder and he around her waist in turn. "I hope you don't mind," she said, with a hint of embarrassment, "it's just that I'm so wasted, and the woods are so dark."

"That's what I'm here for," the boy said, and was careful to not make any false steps in the shadows.

They walked deeper and deeper. A flashlight beaconed out to them in the distance, briefly, but then disappeared. Allie talked to the boy about life at college, about life upstate in the valley. The boy had just arrived the week before. He was from the city, and wasn't yet used to all the tall trees.

"Where I live, you can't see the stars," he said. "The skies are bright at night from the city below." The boy looked down at his feet and held Allie as she walked. "I've never seen the country . . . I've never seen the woods."

"This is where I am," she said, walking briskly. "This is where I'm from."

"From the valley?"

Allie upturned the corners of her lips and wondered if the boy could see it. "Where else?"

"There are a lot of places in the world," he said, in nearly a whisper. "The valley here is just one of many."

Allie stopped and looked at him, her eyebrows raised as if in disbelief. "What?" the boy asked, and then she laughed at him, her mouth opening wide to laugh louder as she went. The woods hushed in silence as she stopped, and then rose to meet her—with the crickets and the frogs and all the creatures left unseen.

"What?" he asked again. "What are you laughing at?"

"Nothing," she said, smiling in the laughter's wake. "I'm laughing at nothing."

They walked further in the flush of the moonlight, and soon Allie was asking him of Rachel: "Who is Rachel? How did you get a girlfriend, your second week at school?"

"I knew Rachel from high school," he said, and was still looking at his feet. "She's been going here a year now, and I decided to join her, just to be close."

"That's so sweet," Allie said, grinning as she held herself to him. "She must be a very lucky girl to have a guy so sweet."

Allie tripped on a rock. She gasped as she grabbed and held to his stomach. The boy held her gently by the shoulder to keep her from falling. "You okay?" he asked.

"I'm fine now," she said, and looked at him considerately. "Thanks."

They walked on, but slowly, with no rushed footsteps. The boy was quiet. He was still watching the ground, and when Allie asked him what he was thinking, he told her that the woods sounded alive.

"They *are* alive," she said. "They always are." The boy remained quiet. Allie could hear the sounds of their footsteps: they crunched in the leaves and padded on pine, leveled on stones and slipped quickly on inclines.

"What were you doing, waiting for Rachel tonight?" Allie asked. "Why wasn't she with you?"

The boy took a deep breath. "She told me she'd meet me … She told me she'd come."

"How long were you waiting, before I showed up?"

The boy smiled, in spite of himself. "Too long."

Allie looked up at him, and her eyes, green, were visible in the moonlight. " … I've been waiting, too, you know."

"How long?" he whispered.

Allie slowed in the darkness and whispered back to him, too. "Longer than you think."

Allie's hand held him close, and after some time, she could feel him holding her closer, still — could feel him relying more upon her than she upon him. And so, Allie guided him. Allie knew how difficult the woods were to navigate at night, if you didn't know better. It was what she had expected; it was what she had counted on.

Allie brought the boy by the river's edge. Being unable to see the water through the trees in the pallid moonlight, it looked to Allie as though the boy never knew. Allie never said anything, and so they walked on, the boy apparently oblivious to it all. They came close to campus, and soon Allie could feel the boy's breath hot upon her shoulder — could feel his heart pump hard in the pounding humidity. He looked in her eyes and asked for her name:

"What is your name?"

"It doesn't matter."
"What do you mean?"
 But it didn't matter.

PART I

O poplar, you are great
among the hill-stones,
while I perish on the path
among the crevices of the rocks.

– Mid-Day, by H.D.

I

"What exactly is a 'dosa'?"

IT'S ALWAYS FUNNY WHEN I get questions like that. All I do, every single time, 100% of all cases, I just repeat back to them what it says on the menu, just verbatim. Large, paper-thin crepe, huge, literally about this big (that's when I spread my hands open about a foot and a half, but they never believe me until they see it for themselves), gets wrapped with your choice of filling, etc. etc. Freakin' *exactly* what it says on the menu, word for word, but somehow it clears up everything.

"How does it taste?" she asks.

"Sour," I say. "Kinda salty. It's made of a kind of fermented rice and lentil batter."

She mulls this over for a while and eventually decides on the spinach dosa with cheese: a Sag Paneer Dosa.

"How would you like that spiced?" I ask. "Mild, medium or hot?"

"Ummm … I don't know … what's the medium like?"

"Well, uhhh … the mild's pretty mild … and the hot's pretty hot … so I guess it's kinda in between. You know?"

My mind sags some days, like a soggy dosa. The kind of people who come into Indian restaurants either love foreign food or their own sense of worldliness. Pseudo-intellectuals and hipster-college know-it-all's. They take it the worst. Whatever. I guess it'll come out of my tip.

"Medium's fine," she says softly, and the tone underscored by her breath says all the rest.

"Sounds good," I say, and take the menus and get out of there before I garner any more contempt than I've already earned.

I go to the back and put up the ticket. "What's the spicing on this?" Tony, the cross-eyed cook asks. "I can never read yer damn handwriting."

Write the ticket for the garlic naan. Put it up. Tell the prep chef. Make sure he heard me, but don't make it sound condescending. Go to the salad server; get out the coconut chutney. Papadams? Already brought that out. So I go and sit in the booth in the back and pick up where I left off.

Saturday lunch shifts are either crazy or dead cause I'm the only one here. They pass intermittently. Two tables here, an hour of total silence there. Sometimes four or five tables will come in at once — that's when I really get screwed — but right now's silence time, and the dining room is dark with dim lighting and quiet except for the sitar playing over the speakers. I sit there in my Indian-style booth (we call them "divans") and am about to go back to reading the book I brought with me when I see one of the candles has gone out. I get up and walk over to one of the five cubbies lining the far left wall. Set back on the inside, a small Shiva statue is dancing *tandava* on top of a dwarf in a ring of fire. A customer once told me that that's his dance of destruction. Shiva dances on the dwarf of ignorance and the universe self-destructs, but he looks pretty content with it, a sly smile implying transcendence, I suppose, but I think that's kind of silly. If he's so transcendent, then why the dance?

I light the candle and watch as the light plays shadows on the flame in his left hand, the drum in his right, when I notice that someone dotted his forehead with a grain of rice plastered to some red gunk in what I guess is supposed to pass for a vermilion mark. I look over at the next cubby and see that someone did the same to Ganesh the elephant god too. I consider cleaning them off but think the better of it. Somehow, it fits. I look back at Shiva, but he only smiles complacently; all's well that ends well, I guess.

I'm just about to go back to my book for the second time when I hear somebody walking up the stairs at the front. Maybe they're just reading the menu at the door. I hate it when people come in, but of course they do anyway.

The door opens and the girl who walks in is skinny, but has big, round eyes, and nice, kind of messy dark brown hair. She's smiling.

"Hi," I say as I walk up toward the front. She rests her hands up on the front counter and doesn't say anything but only continues to smile naturally, her lips shut but pressing dimples deep into her cheeks. I ask her if she wants to sit at a table or at an "Indian-style" divan.

"Oh," she says, as if that says it all. She looks at the divan by the front window, with the table and its short-cropped legs and its raised seating. "Indian-style?" But then she walks over and takes off her shoes. I take that as my cue and I follow her with the menu and am back with the water a moment later.

"How are you?" she asks as I pour her glass full.

"I'm pretty good, thanks. And yourself?"

The girl turns to look at me. "Did you know it's ninety-five degrees outside?" I pause, somehow not knowing what to say. The girl looks at me with her eyes focusing into me like bright spotlights, but still, she's smiling. "That's nineteen degrees warmer than yesterday." Finally those eyes of hers close and her lips fade imperceptibly to a frown, the dimples in her cheeks passing into memory like mist. She shakes her head, as if she's looking at something behind those eyelids happening on the other side of the globe. "The whole world is spinning off its axis."

"And here I was thinking we were coming *out* of summer." I wait for a reply but she only continues to stare through her closed eyes. Weirdo.

I hear the bell ringing from the back, so I walk to the kitchen and get the food ready. Malai Kofta goes with the brown rice; organic brown basmati rice for just a dollar extra. Sag Paneer Dosa goes with the sambar and the chutney, in the little tin bowls. The Sag Dosa is medium spiced, of course.

I bring the food out to the table. The college girl's resumed her airs of contrived haughtiness. She looks at me, disaffected. Oh, the food is here? I suppose that means it is time for me to eat then.

" …And a Sag Dosa with Paneer for you, coconut chutney on the side. Yeah, those dosas are huge, aren't they? Yeah, I wasn't kidding. All right, so does everything look all right? Great. If you folks need anything else at all, just let me know, okay? Enjoy your meal!"

I return to my booth in the back and read my book for a minute or two. *Death in Venice*, by Thomas Mann. It's basically about this conservative, respected writer guy named Aschenbach, who goes walking one day when he sees this red-haired crazy-looking guy in front of a church smiling at him; then he runs away from his old life to Venice where he falls in love with a little boy named Tadzio. My literature professor says it has something to do with "the problem of the artist" and the "amorality of aesthetics," but I kinda think that my literature professor must have his head up his ass or something, because I don't see what pedophiles have to do with artists. My eyes scan the words on autopilot, but really I'm thinking about how weird German people are, when I glance up at the girl sitting at the front by the window. She looks like she still has her eyes closed, but instead of frowning, now she's tapping her fingers on the table, her head bobbing along to her own self-constructed beat. I get up and head to the front to see if she's ready to order.

"Oh!" she says, looking up at me with wide, distracted eyes. "—do you have a restroom?"

"Uh, of course," I say. "Just there in the back on the left."

The girl considers this and nods her head, looking emptily out at what would be the distance if there weren't a wall in her way. She jerks her head to face me all at once, as if she didn't know I was there. "I'm sorry, can I have a small tomato coconut soup and…oh, uh…those crackers?"

"The papadams?"

"Oh, I don't know. They usually come out with those little round glass jars…"

"Yes, of course," I say. "Those come out complimentary."

"Okay," she says. She looks down briefly at the menu facing her the wrong way and hands it to me. "That's it, then."

Side dishes. The side-order customers are barely even worth the effort. Not much in it for me other than a two-dollar compulsion, but I smile anyway. She is pretty cute, after all. I like the way that her hair is kinda messy, yet still looks good with her; but then I remember the way she looked at me with her eyes before, and how they focused in on me as if she were looking straight through me, and feel kind of unsettled. I turn toward the kitchen and walk back with the menu only to see that she's trailing just behind me. I turn briefly to see if she wants something, but deduce by her distant smile that she's barely aware I'm there. Probably heading to the bathroom.

I head to the back and put up the ticket.

"Whaddya got for me this time?" Tony asks. He's doing yoga in front of the stovetop, his knees bent and his arms extended as he practices deep breathing. "Warrior pose," he says.

"Just a side order," I tell him.

"What, no entree?"

"That's right."

"You sure they don't want a bread or nothing? No entrees at all?"

"No entrees, Tony."

"Ah, what the hell. Stab it."

I go back up front with some water and check on my first table, with the medium-spiced girl. "So how's your food?" I ask, putting on my best smile. They murmur back some affirmative response. "How about that dosa? Is the spicing okay?"

"Neither cold nor hot, but lukewarm."

"I'm sorry?"

"The spicing's fine," she finally says, but somehow with reluctance.

"Okay," I say, "great." And I give them one last mandatory nod before heading to the back to get the papadams and the soup to bring out to the girl in the front.

When I come back out the girl has her legs stretched comfortably under the table. I set everything down and make some polite comment or another and am about to go back to my little booth with my book when she speaks again.

"What's your name?" she asks warmly. I turn back to face her because I was already on my way out and see that she's looking at me again, the same way that she looked at me before when her eyes were like spotlights. They're shining into me, I can see.

"My name's Sean," I say. "Sean Vitoff."

She closes her eyes again and nods her head before opening those eyes of hers again and looking at me with a wide, bright smile. "My name is Olivia," she says. I'm about to give her a 'nice to meet you' and maybe even a handshake, but she just goes straight to her papadams, apparently considering the introduction through, so I leave.

Kind of a weird name, Olivia. The kind of name I'd expect an old lady to have, like Mildred or Agatha or something.

In my booth in the back I do some more reading, but I'm getting a little bit confused. The formerly respectable Aschenbach is wandering around Venice — sick with cholera while he stalks after little fourteen-year-old Tadzio — when all of a sudden some unnamed guy starts talking about beauty and Eros to some other guy named Phaedrus. I guess Aschenbach's daydreaming or something, but who the hell is Phaedrus, and who's talking to him? I skim the rest of the section—some nonsense about form and innocence leading to "intoxication and desire" or something—but this literary stuff is always over my head. I think the people who like these kinds of books only pretend to so they can look smarter.

I feel like just stopping altogether but see that there's only three pages left and decide to just trudge along anyway. Eventually Aschenbach stops daydreaming about the unnamed guy and Phaedrus and watches beautiful little Tadzio get beat up by some big stocky kid named Jaisu before Aschenbach finally dies from his cholera. And that's the end.

Stupid book.

I get up and head toward the front. Olivia has her hands resting quietly in her lap as she looks out the window, watching the heat rise.

"All finished with that soup?" I ask.

She turns to face me slowly. I can see the dimples in her cheeks again, and her words come lightly and without malice. "It was very nice, Sean."

"Good, I'm glad you liked it. You sure you don't want anything else, or should I just prepare the check for you?"

"The bill's just fine."

I come back a moment later and place the check on the table and start clearing her dishes and am about to head back when she starts talking to me again.

"May I have your phone number, Sean?"

I was already on my way back and nearly trip when my foot catches on the chair behind me.

"I'm sorry, my what?"

"I was wondering if I could have your phone number."

The most embarrassing part of the whole thing, even more embarrassing than having medium-spiced girl and her whole table listening in on everything, is that I actually blush. My whole face goes red, and I can feel it so obviously that it makes me furious at myself. But Olivia hardly notices, it seems, although her eyes have never left mine. It takes me a few seconds to kind of collect myself and formulate a coherent response: I tell her that I have a girlfriend.

"Really?" She sounds genuinely pleased. "What is her name?"

"Um…Allie."

"Ah," she says, raising up her head. "Allie. I know an Allie. Allie Donowitz?"

"Yeah, that's her actually. So … you know her?" I'm looking for an escape, any way out of this situation, but she just keeps right on talking as if there isn't one thing even the slightest bit awkward about all this.

"Yes, I know her," she says a bit lowly. Finally her eyes drift away from mine. Her face itself never moves, but her eyes shift and I can see her bite her lips tentatively. Olivia mutters something under her breath. Something about cats, maybe, but I can hardly tell.

"I think you misunderstood me, Sean," she says, looking back at me again. She takes an unused napkin from across the table. "Do you have a pen?" I give her mine and she writes down a phone number before sliding both the napkin and the pen toward me with her hand. I pick up the napkin and examine the phone number. When I look up, I see that she's smiling again. But it's never teeth-revealing, never joyful … but somehow … it's calm. It's just there.

"You might have to call me in the near future, Sean."

"I might need to call you?" I ask, looking over the phone number. "Why?"

"Just trust me when I say that everything's going to be okay."

I stand there, holding the napkin like an idiot, and before I can even manage anything out, Olivia gets up. She gets up, slips on her shoes, and heads right for the door. She opens it and walks out, but before she leaves she stops and stands in the threshold, looking outside before somehow thinking the better of it and turning to face me one last time. She's smiling again, but this time it's somehow sad. I want to say something—anything—but find myself unable to even murmur a goodbye.

"See you, Sean." She waits, looking at me with her wide, staring eyes—as if somehow expecting me to say something back—but then, she's gone. Just like that.

Later on, when I'm closing up, the phone starts ringing, and when I pick up it's Allie, calling to see how I'm doing. I tell her that I'm fine. She tells me that she just called to say hi—that she's looking forward to tonight. Cause today's our one-year anniversary. I tell her I'm looking forward to it too.

"I love you, Sean."

"Love you too."

2

I MET ALLIE THE SAME night Lily dumped me. Or at least the same night I finally was able to admit to myself that she had dumped me. Lily was a tall girl, as tall as me, and she had the loudest laugh. She used to laugh at everything, whether you were joking or not. She cursed and swore, and liked to drink a lot too, although she never went to bars or even to parties. I think the only night I ever even saw her out of her house was the night she dumped me.

The only reason I ever met Lily is because I work with Steve, one of her housemates. She lived in a whole house full of hippies. They all used their old bathwater to flush their toilets, but I never complained. I figured it just meant they were living by what they believed, and that was good enough for me. The first time I went over was to smoke a blunt with Steve after work; Lily was there on the couch when we lit up.

Lily was lying down on the couch, wrapped up in a patchwork quilt as she took her first drag. She moved her feet a little to let me sit at the far end, but after she got a little high she put her feet on my lap and started wiggling her toes. She thought that was hilarious, but back then I didn't know she thought everything was, and just figured her for high.

Lily wiggled her big toe in my face. "This little piggy went to the market." Her little toe. "This little piggy went home." She laughed and laughed until her coughing stopped her. Then she brought out a bottle of rum and made us take swigs all around.

I don't know what I saw in her. Who can say? Almost every time I saw her I was drunk. I don't know if I ever saw her sober, except for maybe the mornings, I guess, but by then I was always hung over.

But I do remember that first night we slept together—it was the first night we met. Steven, our mutual friend, had passed out in the corner, snoring so loudly we could barely hear our own voices. Lily thought that was funny too, and sat up and scooted over next to me so we could hear each other speak.

"I've always wanted to travel," she said. "I went to Russia last year and it was just the most amazing experience of my whole life."

"Really?"

"Yeah, man. Just … *fuck*! You don't know how *stupid* we are until you travel. Americans, I mean. We're all so close-minded, just living in a goddamn box."

"If you could go anywhere, where would you go?"

"Oh, man … MONGOLIA!"

"Mongolia?" We both broke out laughing and she lightly slapped my shoulder before continuing.

"Did you know it's one of the emptiest countries in the world? Totally empty. You could go out there and not know what century you're in. You could see Genghis Fucking Khan, man."

Then we had a typical stoner conversation about how messed up it would be if we were walking along in the countryside and suddenly happened to run into Genghis Khan and his horsemen, riding along upon the empty, expansive steppes. And we laughed about that for some time.

"I want to go *everywhere*," she said. "Someday I'm gonna marry some rich, silver-spooned asshole and divorce him, just so I can take his money and go everywhere. Morocco, Thailand, the motherfuckin' *Serengeti*, man!"

"Oh man, I want to go to Morocco so badly."

"Really?"

"Yeah."

"You can go there by taking a boat over from Gibraltar. That's the cheapest way, I looked it up. Anyway, the ferry takes you to Tangier. It used to be an international port city, where all the superspies like James Bond and shit used to hang out. So even today it's supposed to be a pretty messed up place."

"Wow."

"You and I should go to Morocco together."

"Like *Almost Famous*, right?"

Lily screeched in laughter at that one. "YES!" she said. "Yes!" She poured me another shot that I promptly took.

"It's not a bad idea though, when you think about it," she said later. " —take up completely different names, become completely different people. Only we should take it a step further. We should go around the world, and every country we get to, we start over. New names, new personas."

"It could be a game," I said, "thinking up roles to play."

"The best kind of game there is," she said, looking at me.

"We could be lovers."

"Lovers, adulterers … divorcees … even arch-nemeses."

"Sounds like fun."

We stopped talking for a moment. A *Seinfeld* kind of awkward silence, I suppose, unless you count Steve's snoring in the corner, trying to cover it up and make it something different, but to no avail. She was playing with her hair, looking at me. I was just lying back, looking at her too. I grinned and she grinned too, and for once, she didn't laugh. She leaned in, laid herself on top of me and kissed me. I kissed her back and put my hands on her, ran them up and down her back and along her sides. She wasted no time in pulling up the quilt to cover us, wasted even less time in reaching down into my pants with her cool, balmy hands.

I don't think we ever did manage to find our way out of all of our clothes. I think I was still wearing my socks when it was over. They were mismatched. One was pink from being put in the wash with a red tee-shirt of mine, and I'm glad the quilt was covering us up, because otherwise I probably would've looked kinda silly.

Lily looked better clothed than she did naked. Her breasts hung in a weird way, her nipples pointing off toward the sides, giving me mixed signals. Later, we fell asleep in the same position, with her on top, her arms wrapped around me. Her head was on my shoulder, and I could feel her breathing against my skin. She smelled like incense; like sandalwood.

That's basically how things went with Lily and I. Every two or three days I'd stop by and we'd just accelerate from there. She had something about the bathroom that she really liked. Whenever we woke up the next morning, she'd shoo me out of bed or the couch or wherever and have me take a shower with her. It didn't even have to be sexual. Sometimes she'd make a warm bath, sit in the back, have me sit in front of her, and she'd shampoo my hair like I was a little kid again. She'd laugh and laugh about it. Thought it was hysterical. And then later she'd get out of the bath, pee, and wash it down with a fresh bucketload.

I thought I was in love with her. I liked that she didn't own a handbag. That her hair was frizzy and crazy and that she never even made an attempt to tame it. The way she held her cigarettes when she laughed.

Things went on like that for about a month, when one drunken night I told her I loved her. I never would've said that had I been sober. I'm not nearly that stupid.

I didn't get a response at first. Eventually she laughed, but we never spent another night together. No more drunken nights, no more baby-bath mornings.

It took me a long time to accept what had happened. Actually, it was only about a week or two, I guess, but you know how it is. The first two days passed and she didn't call me. I called her the third day. I asked her how she was, she said okay. I asked her if she wanted to hang out later, she said she had plans, blah blah blah. It basically went on like that until I begged Steve to talk to her for me. He did, and said that she would be calling me up real soon about it—that we would set things straight. A few more days passed, nothing happened, and then that weekend I went to the bar and saw Lily there, dancing with her girlfriends, completely plastered, laughing hysterically. And she was in a *bar*, for Christ's sake, I couldn't believe it. Since when did she leave the house? Of all the places I could've seen her—a *bar*.

Looking back on it, I think I fell more in love with the idea of her than with her actual self. I had never slept with a girl on the first night before. And she was just so, I don't know, *herself*, so *different*. I felt like I'd never meet another girl like her, and I liked the idea of being with a girl like that. I could overlook things like her constant coughing, her skewed breasts. I used to imagine marrying her and taking her on a honeymoon around the world. Imagine us assuming roles. One country she'd be a hotel heiress, the next an exotic dancer. But I guess in the end she was just herself.

And now she was at a bar, and she was laughing. Always with her laughing.

Thank God I wasn't stupid or drunk enough to go up to her and say something. What little wounded male dignity I had left I used to keep myself glued to the bar, refusing to even look in her direction. I sat there fuming, imagining her noticing me at the bar, coming over to say hi. I imagined throwing my drink in her face and telling her off, but that's the sort of thing only a girl can do and get away with, and that annoyed me even more. Any action a girl takes in the same situation is indiscriminately accepted, but guys are left shafted. I even considered trying to find some drunk girl to parade around in front of her, but knew now that it wouldn't even make her jealous, and that only got me angrier.

Eventually, when I did manage to get myself out of there, that's when I bumped into Allie—literally. She was even drunker than I was. Was going on about having to go back to campus without her friends and not wanting to go alone through the woods, but I didn't feel like dealing with it.

"Want me to call you a cab?" I asked, but she said she didn't have any money, and I realized I didn't have any either. I dimly realized that that meant I had probably just pissed away fifty bucks at the bar, but just shrugged and told her I was walking back to campus anyway, and that she could walk back with me.

She was so drunk. Just completely falling all over herself, tripping on stuff, so I helped her out by letting her kind of hang on to me as she walked, but honestly, I couldn't have been bothered. Even with a girl like Allie, I just couldn't think about anything else. When I was at the bar I was angry, but by the time we got to the path through the woods I was just depressed and felt like whining. I just wanted to whine and moan to the whole world about how much my life sucked, wanted to lament to this random stranger who kept trying to egg me on into a conversation, wanted to cry and dig myself a hole to die in. Mostly, I just wanted to go to sleep.

"Soo, you live on campus?"

"Yeah."

"And you went to the bar allll by your lonesome?"

"Yeah."

Didn't take her long to catch on, though, I guess. "Is there something wrong?" she finally asked.

"I don't mind," I said.

"No—I mean with you."

I audibly sighed. "Yeah," I said. "I'm fine."

She said nothing for a minute or so. I noticed that her walk was beginning to steady itself.

"What's her name?" she asked later on.

I turned to her and saw her looking straight at me in the moonlight. Had me pegged, I guess.

"Lily."

"What happened?"

"She dumped me a week ago," I said plainly. "Didn't bother to notify me, though." I looked at Allie and only saw her staring straight ahead, away from me. I noticed she was loosening her hand from my waist.

"I'm sorry," I said. "It's just been a bad night for me." Allie looked at me and smiled with a kind of a resigned shrug. What could she do? In her own way, she was letting me know that everything was okay.

A minute later Allie stopped and let go of me. She was rubbing her face with her hands.

"Sobering up?" I asked.

"Yeah," she said. She let her arms sway a bit at her side. "Mind if we take a break for a minute?"

I sat back against some tree and neither of us said a word for some time. I couldn't stop thinking about Lily—about the smell of sandalwood—about how it felt like to go to sleep with her in my arms—how it felt like to have her wash my hair—to lay back in the bathtub and have her breasts cushion my back while she laughed.

And then suddenly I realized that I didn't have a single thing in my possession that signified the relationship I had had with her. No pictures, no keepsakes. She never came to my place. Her scent didn't carry to my blankets. I'd go back to my room, and the fan would be going, the moon would be shining in through the window, the floor would be clean, and Ivan's goddamn dehumidifier would be on. And I'd be alone in my bed, as if the last month had never even happened.

"I think I know your Lily," Allie said abruptly.

"Huh?" I asked, raising my head.

"Black, frizzy hair, right?" I nodded silently. Allie shook her head. "I'm sorry about what happened," she said. "I've seen her do it before, to a lot of guys." Great. So now I wasn't even a unique guy to have been shat on, but just another part of a patterned sequence of shatting. I wondered if maybe *my* scent would linger on that patchwork quilt of hers.

"Just for once I would've liked to have seen it happen the other way around," she said, and looked off in the distance.

I got up and brushed off my pant legs. "Ah," I said, "fuck her."

Allie smiled and got up too. "You know, I don't think I ever got your name."

"Sean Vitoff," I said. "Nice to meet you."

She laughed. "My name's Allie. Very nice to meet you, too."

It's crazy how fast she seemed to sober up that night, but she walked the rest of the way back just fine with her hands loosely at her sides, as if she hadn't even drank that night at all. She talked to me about how she grew up in the area. About how there's a lot of interesting places, once you know where to look.

"Like up in High Falls they have a whole network of caves you can go in. They also have this railway trestle that they turned into a walking bridge. It's really high up, something like two hundred feet, and it goes over Roundout Creek through a little valley there. There's a lot of beautiful stuff up by Lake Minnewaska, too. Lots of waterfalls … but I guess you kinda have to be into that sort of stuff to appreciate it."

It wasn't long till we finally reached the dorms. We kind of just stood there a moment. She was going this way, I was going that, but in the meantime we were just kind of standing.

"So, are you okay now?" I asked, "or am I gonna have to walk you to your door too?"

She laughed. "I think I'll be okay … but it was a nice walk. It was what I needed."

"Yeah, me too."

Allie put her hands in her pockets — looked off at the moon for a moment, back at me again.

"So … "

" — You deserve better than Lily, Sean." I tried to hide it, but I blushed. I always blush at the stupidest times. "I mean that."

"Thanks," I said, not knowing what else to.

"Here, listen," she said. Allie approached me and took a pen out of her pocket. She gently took my hand and wrote her number on it. "In case you ever want to see any of those places we talked about … you know, like the railway trestle."

I smiled. "What about the caves?"

Allie put her hands on her hips and looked at me coyly. "That's fun too." She smiled. "Goodnight," she said, and left without another word.

I didn't call her until about a week later. I know that's breaking the rules or whatever, but really, Allie wasn't much on my mind. I was still on my post-Lily hangover and mostly hated the female race for a few days.

Allie really is just the most gorgeous girl, though, and almost archetypally so. That's the thing I never really understood, because we really do look like a kind of mismatched couple. Not that I'm ugly or anything, but any guy short of a Brad Pitt type would look mismatched next to Allie. I figured she wasn't really interested in me, and if she was at the time, it was on account of the alcohol; but eventually I called her anyway. Even though that was just the worst night for me, I did like her. I liked the fact that she wasn't prissy or stuck-up; that she talked to me naturally, as if she knew me already. Behind her looks, she seemed like just another local girl who liked waterfalls and mountains. And as much as I didn't want to admit at the time, she did kinda cheer me up that night. She made me blush.

"Hello?"

"Hey, uh, this is Sean. We, uh, I was the ... "

"—Hey, Sean! How are you?"

The first place we went to ended up being the railway trestle after all. And it's funny—it was so nearby. A ten-minute drive, maybe? By then, I had already been living in the valley for nearly three years. It made me wonder how insulated campus life really is from everything else out there. I wondered what more I was missing.

When we first pulled into the parking lot—which was little more than a gravel clearing off the side of the road—it didn't look like there was anything around at all. A random-looking church across the street, an anonymous-looking path leading into the woods, but otherwise, not much to signal what was ahead. The path from the lot went into the woods, deep into the green, and walking along what looked to be a path like any other, suddenly the walkway cut forward on a bridge while the land dropped away into a gorge below. The land dropped away surreptitiously—almost secretly. Even then, it was hard to tell how high up we really were—until the path jutted out from above the tree tops—far above the houses and the road and the river flowing on below.

When we got there it was late in the afternoon, and the sun was down low, just above the hilltops, casting golden light on the bright green trees. I walked as far along the path as you could; about halfway across the bridge, the walking path ends abruptly with a built-up wooden barrier, and on the other side are the remnants of the old railway bridge that the path was built upon. Looking out from there at the rest of the old railway bridge was like looking at a skeleton, and I didn't realize how old the bridge was underneath me until I saw all the rotting wood out past the barrier. I looked over the edge and tossed a penny to see how far down the drop was. It bounced off some rusty iron girders and fell a long, long way before ever reaching the river below.

"Hurl your green over us," Allie said, looking down at the river and the trees. "Cover us with your pools of fir."

"What's that now?" I asked. "Poetry or something?" But Allie just smiled knowingly and pointed to one red house down below on the riverside.

"What's that?" I asked, and she told me a story about how once a few years back the dad who lived there told his wife and kids to watch him as he went up on the bridge; he said he had a surprise to show them.

"Anyway, the story goes that he came up here, climbed up on the railing here on the edge, and waved down to all of them. They all waved back, and then he jumped and killed himself, right in front of them all."

"No way," I said. "You're lying."

"Nuh uh," she said. "True story. That red house right down there. And he jumped from right here." Allie tapped the wooden railing with her hand and smiled just slightly. I craned my body over the railing this time, looking all the way down, letting the vertigo embrace me as I imagined falling, imagined the wind on my face before I hit the water. Somebody once told me that when people jump like that, they die before they hit the bottom from a heart attack or something. I hope that's not true, because if I wanted to kill myself by jumping off a bridge, I'd at least want the pleasure of the experience before I died.

"It's so high," I said, then got dizzy and felt like I actually was falling, and backed away from the edge.

"Check this out," Allie said, and then climbed over the edge of the walking bridge onto the old railway trestle beyond. On the actual walking path there was sturdy wood, and you couldn't tell by looking down what lay underneath it, just the same as a boardwalk on a beach. But past the path on the old trestle there were wooden beams going across with almost a foot of empty space in between. The look down was a constant reminder of how far you had to fall.

"Oh God," I said, watching her as she took a few steps out onto the trestle. "That's crazy."

"Come on," she said, waving with her hand for me to follow. She motioned her head out toward the other end of the trestle, where it went further into the woods on the other side of the gorge. "Climb over the barrier!"

"Oh God." I climbed over the barrier as slowly as I could, and still held to it as I stepped onto the first rotting wooden beam.

"Come on," she said, with her hand extended, her smile grinning. "It's not that bad."

"But what if you trip?" I asked, and she explained to me how the gaps between the beams were too small to actually fall through.

"Worse comes to worst, you get your foot snagged and sprain your ankle."

"Great," I said. "That makes me feel loads better."

It took me a while to get used to it. I would take a few steps out, run back, few more steps out, run right back, but eventually I managed to make my way out to her. The key was to only look at the next beam I had to step on, and never at the gaps in between. Because the moment I remembered how high up I was, that'd be the moment I'd lose my head.

Eventually we got pretty far—we could start to make out the overgrown path through the woods on the other side. And for the first time since I had climbed over, I finally stood still on the beams, my arms outstretched and balanced by my side. The gorge opened out before me like a wide, bellowing breath, carving through the steep, rocky hills on both sides. The river glistened in the sunlight like a white wire curling through the bottom of the gorge, set there as if to mark the way. I was so high; I had no guardrail to hang on to. I looked ahead at Allie, laughing on the beams, near the path through the woods, eager to usher me on to the other side.

But why? What for? To take me across only to reach a tick-infested, overgrown, unused, railroad grade? I looked hard across the way to the path with my eyes squinted to keep myself from feeling dizzy. I looked, but there was nothing out there—grass and underbrush and overhanging trees. What did she want me to see so badly?

"Allie," I said, " —what are we doing here?"

Allie cocked her head at me and appeared not to understand. "What are we doing where?"

"We were fine on the walkway. What's the need to come out here?" But Allie just dismissed me with a wave of her hand.

"We're almost there!" she said, trying to get me excited, but that's when we heard the cops from back down below.

The cops were standing outside of their car, pulled over on the side of the road that flowed beneath the bridge. There were two of them, and the one with the wide-brimmed hat was shouting at us over his PA, telling us to turn back and meet them at the start of the path. I started to turn around, thinking about how I really couldn't afford to pay some stupid summons fee, when Allie grabbed my hand before I could even take my first step.

"Come on!" she said. "This way!" And then she broke into a run, dragging me behind the whole way across.

I don't know how I didn't break my leg or fall or something. She was moving so fast and I was so scared, I could barely even tell my brain to move. I lost all perspective—could only see the gaps, never the beams, the world was spinning, nearly fainted—but before I even knew it, we were across on the other side, and she was laughing.

I fell to my ass and lay down on my back, my heart pumping a buck-fifty.

"Holy shit," I said. "Holy shit."

"That was great!" she said. "Wasn't that great?"

"Yeah," I said, between my panting. "Sure."

We never did end up having to deal with those cops, but in the end I wasn't sure the whole ordeal was worth it anyway. Once I had calmed down enough to look around at where I actually was, I saw that—just as I thought—we were on an old, overgrown, nondescript railroad grade. The path continued ahead, but there was too much brush, and probably went nowhere of interest. Allie looked with awestruck eyes and appeared to be looking at a different scene altogether.

"I've never been here before," she said, and I couldn't believe how much she was smiling. "You have no idea how many years I've wanted to do this."

Not that there was much for us to actually *do*. Eventually—once Allie herself realized there was nothing to see but an overgrown path—she led us down the hill, through the woods down toward the road, and from there it was an easy hike back to the parking lot. Even then, I was still a little worried about the cops being there, but they were nowhere to be found. Allie laughed at how scared I had been at the whole thing.

"We should do this again sometime," she said.

Despite a few hitches, the trestle was only the first of many adventures; and every week, it seemed, Allie would find a new place to take me. One such place was Overlook Mountain, with the ruined remnants of an old luxury hotel at the top on a cliff side. Allie told me it had burned down in a fire a hundred years ago, and in one room I found a huge, moss-covered tree growing out from the corpse of an old, cracked bathtub. We went to other places too: Minnewaska with its stark, white-faced cliffs and back to High Falls again for the abandoned mining caves left hollow beneath the mountains.

At first, there was nothing really romantic about our little trips. I still thought that Allie would never like a guy like me, and because I never really considered it a possibility, I never found myself falling for her. Some people say you can't help falling in love, but I say different. Love doesn't happen by itself; it has to be invited. Not falling for Allie was my defense mechanism.

Eventually Allie and I were going on our little excursions every Sunday. We only bothered calling each other if for some reason one of us couldn't make it, but otherwise, she was right there to pick me up from my dorm every Sunday at eleven in the morning. Even I can appreciate how strangely things evolved between us — the first few times we hung out, Allie barely even talked, and if she did, it was never about herself. Allie liked to explain the history of places to me — how the father had jumped from the bridge a few years back, why there was a Tibetan Buddhist monastery across the street from Overlook Mountain's trailhead and how the Dalai Lama had stayed there — things like that. But what she never told me was her own history: how she had grown up in this valley, with its caves and its ruins; who had first brought her to these places and why she loved them. And she did love them; that much was obvious. She'd show me the ruins and she'd watch me wander and find the tree growing out from the old bathtub and I'd see the affection she had for these places in her eyes. What I guess I didn't see coming was how eventually that affection would turn to me, too. My defenses wouldn't *let* me see that coming, because the moment I allowed myself to even speculate

about things like that, that would be the moment I would be invit-
ing love in. And I wasn't ready for that; Allie had to coax me into it.

Finally, Allie took me to a place she called "Shaft 2A," perhaps the
most isolated place she had yet to bring me. "*Nobody* knows about
Shaft 2A," she told me. "Nobody." It was a fairly long drive to get
there, and we nearly had to leave the valley altogether: about a half
hour over the Shawangunk Ridge (known to locals as "The Gunks");
past the hairpin turn Bob Dylan crashed his motorcycle on in '66; past
Lake Minnewaska, even, edging on toward the Catskills.

"I've heard some people also call this place 'the stockade,'" she said.

"The stockade? Why do they call it that?"

Allie shrugged. "What's in a name?"

When we arrived, it was hard for me to imagine how anybody
could find a place like Shaft 2A unless they knew where to look for it.
Passing run-down trailers, shacks, and even old rock quarries, Shaft
2A was miles off the main road, the entrance at the fenced-off dead
end of an obscure dirt road.

"This is it?" I asked when she stopped the car.

"This is the beginning."

I got out of the car and examined the wooden gate blocking the
way. It was anonymous and bolted, but not locked shut. In fact, it
wasn't even wide enough to block the whole road, but only enough
to block cars from driving through it. Remembering the cops on the
railway trestle, I scanned the area with my eyes, looking for signs,
but couldn't find any — no trespassing or otherwise. Allie got out
of the car and joined me at the gate, regarding me with humor, as if
sensing my skepticism.

"This place used to be an old shale-mining pit," she said, her hand
resting on the wooden gate, "but nowadays it's abandoned."

"Well, enough people know about it to call it the stockade, at least."
Allie smirked and began to walk around the gate. "Right?"

"Right," Allie said, smiling. "And how do you know I didn't make
up that name just now?"

Meeting her eyes, I joined Allie and walked around the gate with
her. "I guess I don't," I said.

Like the railway trestle, the beginnings of Shaft 2A were anonymous and discrete, nothing but an old gravel road going off into the
woods. But where the land at the trestle dropped away, the land at
the stockade opened up all around us; about a quarter mile in, the

woods gave way to a field, spreading out before us like a revelation—a widening breadth of wind-blown grass and blossoming wildflowers—white and red and purple and bursting.

The field was in a basin, I could see, with a small ridge surrounding it on every side, save for the direction we came. There were dirt paths through the flowers that you could walk through; Allie was leading me through them all. She'd crouch delicately by little white starbursts and pronounce to me their names: Stars of Bethlehem, letting their tips linger upon her fingers; Slender Ladies' Tresses, growing on green stalks, white flowers wreathing around them in elongated, basal clusters.

"Who invented these names?"

"Someone wonderful," she said, "—to look upon these wonders and give them such fitting names."

The flowers soon passed, and what was left in their wake was the old shale-mining pit Allie described to me before. The place looked like it had been abandoned years ago: black and brown rocks were strewn carelessly and flowers bloomed where they could, and off on the edge, near the ridge, was a bulldozer left for dead. Allie guided me by the hand, leading me down the dirt paths as they wound through the flowers and the rocks—past withered patches of sun-blanched milkweed and crumbling piles of disintegrating rubble—all the while keeping our destination a well-kept secret. I followed her with ease, holding her hand as she let me, and somehow, I was surprised. Allie didn't seem like the kind of person who held peoples' hands—and yet she was holding mine. And then Allie looked at me, as if somehow sensing my thoughts. She smiled. *I know*, her smile said. *I know*. Until then, she had held my hand only once, and only then to keep me moving over the railway trestle, with the cops and their PA below. Things were different now; things had changed.

Allie craned her neck over the flowers. "Here it is," she said, and then let go of my hand. Somehow, I felt sorry—until I saw where she had brought me: to a helipad, nestled in the bosom of the ridges and the mountains, left there to fade in the passage of time. There wasn't much to it, once I stopped I looked at it: a big square asphalt strip with a yellow painted circle and an "H" in the middle—but there was more to it, somehow—something about the weeds, growing up from the cracks in the old blacktop. Like lost love letters; unread, unrequited, unknown. Why did they need a helipad in a shale-mining pit? Allie and I discussed the possibilities, but neither of us knew. Looking out on the other side of the pit, there was an old electrical generator. What was it all for?

"The stockade is full of secret places," Allie said, smiling as if to say she knew them all.

Allie led the way again: through the flowers, past the shale-mining pit, and into the woods. And once we entered the woods, well, I guess you could say Allie was in her element; it was one thing after another. The trail led us first to a split-open concrete dam, with water pouring through it relentlessly, gushing inexplicably past us to a place we wouldn't follow.

"Where does it go?" I ventured to ask, but Allie just shrugged.

"The ocean," she said, as if it were common sense. "Where does any of it go?"

We crossed the concrete dam, balancing on it precariously, leaping over the gushing split in the middle before following the river upstream on the other side. Walking by the banks for no more than a few minutes, we soon found ourselves traversing a wide river of rocks, the water dispersed across its length in lazy, trickling streams. Leading me further, Allie brought me uphill, the river of rocks taking us up rock staircases, carpeted with wet, dripping moss, the water but rain drizzling from the foliage.

"Where are we going?" I asked.

"Here," she said, and pointed: to the rocks ending abruptly with a natural amphitheater carved out of the sheer, white-faced rock wall; to an immensely tall, hidden waterfall. Looking at it from a distance, it was hard for me to believe that this was all the same stream; at the top of the cliff, the water swooped over the edge in one powerful, narrow, concentrated shot, plummeting a good hundred feet before crashing into the boulders below. Was this the same water that dripped peacefully from the moss that I stood upon? That trickled lazily down the wide river of rocks, only to gush through the dam and lead to the ocean? Was this water really going—to the *ocean*?

Allie and I ambled up to the waterfall and spent some time behind it, in the back of the amphitheater, watching the water come down. The water would flow off from the top, so graceful and free it appeared to not be falling at all; but then I'd follow it with my eyes toward its ultimate trajectory—watch as the water would vaporize into mist as it smashed into the rocks at the bottom. And somehow, in the midst of it all, I thought of the man, on the bridge, waving down to his family in the red, riverside house. How did it feel, to make that leap? At what point does freedom morph into violence, or is freedom violent from the start?

Allie remained silent, and after a few minutes ushered me up a path that took us around the ridge and then all the way around to the top. She led me along the cliff side, following the sound of rushing water, and finally brought me to a rock we could sit on, directly next to where the water flowed down from above.

"We're here," she said. "We made it." And then, as if oblivious to the obvious danger of where we were, Allie sat happily and dangled her feet off the edge of the cliff. My stomach turning a bit as I watched her sit, I stayed back, content to keep myself on solid ground. Sitting there, breathing deeply, it didn't take long for me to appreciate the view; from where we sat, the cliff overlooked the whole of the valley, spread open before us in undulating gradations of green. I could see the helipad from there; I could see the Catskills.

Allie and I just sat there for a while, not saying much of anything, and as the time passed, I began to wonder if Allie would speak to me at all. But then when *did* Allie speak, if not to explain a place to me? There wasn't much history to explain at a place like a cliff side; a ridge was a ridge and a waterfall was a waterfall, and its history was only known to the rocks that had witnessed it. But then, I had thought too soon: Allie would have her say.

"This whole area," she said, "the Catskills, the ridge, all this..." Allie motioned over the land with her hand, as if she knew where all of it went; as if it all belonged to her. "—it all used to be a plateau, and during the ice age was completely frozen over. Hard to imagine, right? Just an endless ocean of ice, covering everything you can see beneath thousands of feet of glaciers. And then the ice age ended." Allie looked out from the cliff side as if this somehow disappointed her. "The glaciers retreated and tore away from the land as it went, and the valley and the mountains here are the ultimate result."

A "dissected plateau" is what she called it, and I couldn't think of a more suitable name. Our valley wasn't even a real valley: it was a valley that had been dissected—torn apart by the forces of history and left exposed as a worn, festering hole. Allie, for her part, stared out at the mountains in silence, watching as the hawks and vultures hovered and circled from above. "Those mountains out there," she said, pointing out to the Catskills, "that's the Devil's Path range of the Catskills. There's this incredible path out there that runs right along the fall line that I've only done parts of, and it's some of the toughest hiking in the whole northeast. We should go there … someday."

"How did you find this place?" I asked abruptly. "I mean, who first brought you here?"

Allie looked at me, almost in surprise. As if I had broken some kind of unspoken taboo.

"I found this place," she said, turning away. She stared off at the mountains again, as if for guidance. "Growing up here, you kind of get to exploring. Sometimes, I just drive, you know, and try to get lost. One of those times … I found the stockade." Allie looked at me knowingly and smiled, even shrugged. "So I made up the name," she said. "What're you gonna do?"

"And Shaft 2A?"

"It's the name of the street. Made sense to me." I laughed, and she just shrugged again. "Anyway, now this place is mine … My own." She swayed her dangling feet in the open air off the cliff side. "The pit and the helipad, the ridge and the waterhole upstream that I've yet to have shown you … this place is my best kept secret."

Allie turned to me and smiled — a subtle, secret smile — unknown to me then, and seeing it only for the very first time. I didn't know what to think. I wanted her to hold my hand, like she did by the wildflowers, but in the end she didn't have to. Her smile was enough.

3

My house looks like a boathouse when you first see it. Anchored to the river flowing endlessly behind it, it has only one floor, its windows round like portholes, its roof but a shallow encasing. Directly behind my house, bordering the river is the rail trail, an old railroad grade laid down with carelessly strewn gravel. The rail trail goes on for about ten miles in each direction and ends eventually on the northern side at the built-up wooden barrier Allie and I conquered and climbed over in High Falls. Right behind my house, the rail trail follows the Wallkill River: a very quiet, pretty river that also sometimes smells. Someone once told me that for over a hundred years they used to pump out all the raw sewage there, and I can believe it. Allie doesn't seem to notice; most times she comes over it's through my backdoor, directly off the trail, wildflowers in her hands. At times I'll find them in my room when I come home from work, set in a vase by the window, put there sometime when I wasn't there. It's all still new to me; I only moved in a few short months ago.

Of course, it was Allie who encouraged me to move off-campus in the first place. Allie regarded the campus with a kind of distaste — she used to compare it to Disneyland and claimed it wasn't really a part of the town.

"Then why do you live here?" I had dared to ask, and Allie looked at me with disdain.

"You know why."

Eventually, after three years of living on a campus she apparently hated, Allie began to consider living in what is colloquially known as "The Orphanage"—a giant dump of a complex housing upward of thirty different college students and probably the worst place to live in town. I thought she was crazy, but on my front, meanwhile, Allie was lobbying heavily for me to move to my current location, once she heard I had found an open house there. It wasn't so much the house, she said, as it was the street, the rail trail and the river behind it. She told me it was the best I could hope for; that in the river lay the true heart of town. "You don't understand, what it means to live on Water Street," she told me, although she's never lived here. "*Such* a beautiful road."

Walking down it now, on my way home from work, I can begin to see what she means. Enclosed on both sides by tall, canopied trees, Water Street snakes along with the river, and—only a half mile off Main Street—my house is the last one on the block. After that, the road crosses the river, leaves it behind, and goes off into the woods on its own. Town ends—but I am still in town.

When I pass the last bend before my house, I see there's no car in the driveway, which means Allie hasn't arrived yet. Maybe I'll have the place to myself for a little while before Allie arrives, just to relax, but then I realize that Ivan's probably around. The house is pretty small, so Ivan's my only housemate. We get along fairly well—he was my old roommate from campus, after all—but somehow I'm not in the mood for him right now and silently hope he's not around.

I walk in and take a spying look around the deserted expanse of the hallway and living room, but hear nothing. Maybe he's out after all, but the moment I walk into my room I hear him calling for me from back down the hall. "Sean?" I hear him call in his thick, Russian accent. "Sean, is that you?"

"Who else would it be?" I call back, and promptly shut the door behind me. Turning around and seeing the old, wood-framed bed, I sigh deeply before lying down in it, allowing my body to sink heavily into its deep, stuffed mattress. I look emptily out in front of me, my eyes wandering aimlessly before eventually resting on the archaic, iron-grated fireplace on the far side of my room. The sun peeks in through my porthole window and casts the naked dust alight in thick, humid beams. Apart from my bed, my dresser, and the ancient iron fireplace, the room is sparse, spartan and spacious, with worn wooden floorboards, scratched up from the furniture of all the people who came before me. It's only a matter of time before Ivan comes back looking for me, I know, but for now I just close my eyes anyway, my arms and legs outstretched, just getting comfortable, when I hear him coming down the hall. "Great," I mutter, and then he's knocking at the door.

"Sean?" he calls. I sigh again and rub my forehead before responding.

"Yeah?"

"May I come in?"

"Yeah, yeah."

The door opens but Ivan only stands in the threshold, looking out at me over his long, imposing nose. Then he looks around my room and takes note of its uncharacteristic cleanliness. "Allie is coming over tonight, I see." I nod and look out at the fireplace again, and he just stands there saying nothing for a few seconds. I look back at him and he's pushing his long black hair behind his ear. Then he's scratching at his beard. "What are your plans tonight?" he asks.

"I dunno."

"You do not know."

"Well, we've got an early start tomorrow morning. Probably not a good idea to stay up late tonight."

"I see." He looks around my room some more. "When is she coming over?"

"Is there something you mean to ask me, Ivan?"

Ivan smirks and crosses his arms before leaning up against the back of my door. "I was just wondering — do you mean to speak with her tonight?" I look up at him and see him looking back, trying to read between the lines in my face. "About her coming to live here, I mean," he says, but there's acid behind his words and he's a fool if he thinks I can't see it.

I look back at the ceiling again, watch the dust and say nothing for a few seconds before replying. "I thought you said you didn't want her living here."

"Actually, I said I did not think it was a good idea. That is different."

"What, and her moving into the Orphanage was a good idea?"

Ivan says nothing. The bastard's still smiling, but I answer him anyway. "I don't know," I finally admit. "I'm not sure I should ask unless I know she'll say yes, you know? I don't want to make a big deal out of it."

"She has been unhappy with her living situation ever since her mother moved away; she might like moving here." Ivan pauses before continuing. "You are too afraid of her."

"Afraid of her?" I balk. "Allie hates her mom, what the hell does that have to do with anything?" Ivan remains silent. "And what do you care, anyway? You're the one who doesn't think it's a good idea."

Ivan smiles with an unexpected warmth. "And I still do not think it is a good idea."

"Dammit, Russki—would you just leave me the hell alone?" But Ivan just laughs and uncrosses his arms.

"I am sorry," he says with a slight bow. "You do what you like, Sean. I will go back to my room." Ivan turns and is about to do just that when I call out for him to stop before he can.

"Vanya," I say. Ivan stops in his footsteps with his back still turned to me.

"If you don't mind her living here," I ask, "then why do you think it's a bad idea?"

Ivan remains silent and still faces out toward the hall. I hear the floorboards creak beneath him before he turns and looks at me, but only for a moment; then he's looking out at my porthole window, but there's nothing out there except the rail trail and the Wallkill beyond it.

"Not a bad idea for you—a bad idea for *her*." He looks back at me again and smiles before leaving. "Just a humble opinion," he says, and shuts the door behind him.

The sound of the shut door reverberates upon the hardwood floor, and suddenly I realize I am all by myself. My eyes remain fixed upon the spot he has just left, and somehow expecting Ivan to return, all I hear are the creaking of the floorboards in the hallway outside—the sound of Ivan leaving me behind.

Laying my head back on the pillows beneath me, I sigh deeply and find myself rubbing my temples with my hands. "Dammit," I hear myself murmur aloud, and somehow, I don't know why, the situation upsets me. I look out the porthole window—as if expecting something to have changed out there in the last few minutes—but there is nothing but afternoon sunlight, as there has been all along. And as I lie thickly in the mattress—staring soundlessly at the light in the window—I feel my mind wander back down blind alleyways and corridors: to the face and voice of Allie, there before me, only last spring.

We had been sitting on the main quad that day, back when we both still lived on campus. It was warm, one of the first warm days of the year, and we were sprawled out on the grass, me in a tee-shirt, and she in her black tank-top. We hadn't been speaking much, until I told her: about here; this place; this house; with the rail trail behind me and the river beyond.

"You found a house on Water Street?" Allie looked up at me with something that approached shock, and I wasn't exactly sure what to think. "Where?"

"I don't know … On the river?" Allie frowned and very nearly rolled her eyes. All the houses on Water Street are on the river. It's why they named it as much. "Not far from Main Street, I guess … maybe a half mile? But it's the last house on the block; once you pass it, the road crosses the river and leaves town."

"*That* house?" Allie asked, apparently knowing just which one. "Sean — you *have* to move there."

"Well, the rent's about twelve hundred a month and … "

" — You don't understand," she said, looking at me with meaning. A kid ran by, screaming and hollering. Apparently he had just caught a frisbee; apparently, this was something worth shouting about. "That house is the best house you could hope for," she continued. "That house and that house alone."

"I don't know," I said, and lay on my back and stared up at the sky. "Ivan and I aren't even sure if we want to move off-campus yet. It's just an idea we're kicking around."

"What, the rent's too much?"

"Well, we were kind of hoping for maybe a third person … " I said, but didn't have the backbone to continue.

Allie leaned on her elbow and lay on her side. "Maybe it is a little bit more than you're paying now. I understand that. But this campus … " Allie looked around — at the frisbee players; at a girl, tanning just down the way. " — this town *isn't* the campus." Allie looked back at me again. "There's *more*," she said, and said it as if it were a promise.

"Then why do you live here?"

Allie shot me a mistrustful glance. She looked away from me, and replied to me in a voice lower than I expected. "You know why."

"Just get a job," I said. "You never go out — you never see *anyone*, at least besides me, and then you live in a single on a campus you hate because you say you can't afford a one-bedroom in the town itself. You don't want to live with other people, but only in a room by yourself, and instead of — god forbid — trying to make friends with somebody out there, you're actually considering moving into the *Orphanage* — of all places, Allie, the Orphanage!"

"I *can't* afford a one-bedroom, Sean," she said, as if I didn't know.

"I'm just saying … " Allie looked at me incredulously, and whatever it was I really wanted to say, I wasn't about to say it. "Just … you don't have to live this way forever."

Allie sighed. She sighed and looked away from me: at the quad, at the grass, at the sky, at the campus in all its well-tended glory. "How else should I live, Sean?" she asked, and I did not have the courage to reply.

"You don't understand, what it means to live on Water Street," she continued, with her stare off in the distance. "The Wallkill, the rail trail, the woods just across the road … " Allie looked up at me, and for the first time in what felt like a long time, she smiled. "It's the heart of this town."

"Then move there with me," I wanted to say, but didn't. "*Please.*"

Allie looked away from me; the conversation was through. "Such a beautiful road," she said, and then repeated it. "Such a beautiful road … "

A bird chirps outside my window, and I hear myself sighing once again. I look about my room: at the iron-grate fireplace; at the minimal furniture and the dust in the air. It's nicer than campus, I suppose. But what real difference does it make in the end?

"Allie," Olivia had said to me, earlier today. "I know an Allie."

Allie, she had said, but *nobody* knows Allie. The more I think about it, the more I realize that Olivia is the first person I've ever met who even knows who Allie *is*. And then she told me I'd have to call her? In the near future? Lying in my bed, I take out the napkin she gave me with the phone number scrawled upon it. It's there, all right, just as I remembered; apparently, I didn't imagine it.

The truth is, I've been meaning to ask Allie about moving in with me for a long time now. I close my eyes and take a deep breath, telling myself that I *would* ask her, if only things were simple—that I'd ask her, if this were any other situation but my own. And that, of course, is when I hear a knock at the door, and this time I know it's her: Allie, coming from elsewhere and abroad, here to my house, for me and for me alone.

"Knock, knock," I hear Allie call from behind my door, and she walks in before I can reply. I quickly stuff the napkin back in my pocket and rise to meet her; Allie gives me a hug before planting a kiss on my cheek.

"Happy anniversary," she says, nearly whispering.

"Yeah," I say, "you too."

I feel a cold weight against my back. We separate, and when I look down I'm surprised to see a bottle of wine in her hand — Pinot Noir. "Wine?" I ask.

"As good an occasion as any, right? *In vino veritas*!" She hands it to me and I look it over. "Why? Something wrong?"

"No," I say, putting it down on my bed. I wrap my arms around her waist and hold her close. "Just … surprised, is all. You never drink."

Allie grins and places a flirtatious finger on my chest. "I did the night we met, didn't I?" And then we both laugh a little.

"Well, yeah, I guess. But I can't remember any other time — ever."

"Well, then you've got tonight to remember me by."

"Right," I say. "Tonight."

Allie lets herself go and tugs a bit at my hand. "Come on," she says. "Help me get the food out of the trunk." So we go outside to her car and I help her unload. Big paper bags, filled with all sorts of stuff: pasta and tomatoes and cream and cooking vodka — which makes sense — then spinach and chard and other leafy vegetables I don't know the names of, a big bag of brown rice and even a bag of apples. "What's all this then?" I ask. "Packing a bit of an extended lunch for the trip tomorrow?"

Allie smiles and takes a bag off my hands. "About time somebody bought you some decent food," she says. I smile back, but secretly wish she got me some bacon or cold cuts or something. Then again, what else can I expect from a vegetarian, even if she is my girlfriend? So I go back to the trunk and find in another bag a whole bottle of Jack Daniels.

"Jesus Christ!" I take the bottle out of the bag and look it over. "What the hell is this?"

"Jack and Coke," she says, smiling. "It's your favorite, isn't it?" But all I can do is shake my head — I can't remember a single other time she's ever gotten me alcohol before. "What?" she asks.

"Nothing," I say, not knowing what else to. "Nothing at all."

I unload one last paper bag and put it on the grass. Allie starts going through them and asks me if that's everything.

"I think so," I say, but that's when I spot a plastic bag from Rite-Aid, still sitting way back in the trunk. I figure maybe she got mosquito repellent or something for tomorrow, until I open it up and look inside. "Whoa," I mutter, like a fool. I look to see if she's watching, but she's still going through the bags, so I put it back quickly before she can see what I found.

"Okay," she says, standing up and brushing her hands off on her hips. "So that *is* it, right?"

"Uh, yeah."

Allie cocks her head at me and all I can do is grin dumbly.

"You're blushing, you know."

"Yeah ... " My voice trails off. " — you *sure* this is everything?" I ask, but it sounds stupider than I thought it would when it comes out of my mouth. Words never sound as good outside my head.

Allie smiles, awkwardly, and looks at me sideways. "What are you talking about?"

"Nothing ... " I say, taking her hands. She looks at me a little bit confused, but then just gives up with a smile and gives me a peck on the lips before motioning me to help her bring everything inside.

"So I've got a plan for us tonight," she says as we set everything down in the kitchen. "After we make dinner and everything, I thought we might enjoy eating in your room." Allie looks up at me from beneath her eyelashes and smiles. "You know, by the fireside."

"Fireside?" I ask, taking a moment to figure out what the heck she even means. When I do, I raise an eyebrow. "In August?"

"We can turn up the AC," she says. " — get it going really cold the whole time we're cooking; then we can light the fire and it'll even things out. What do you think?"

I think it's kind of ridiculous, actually, but I remember what I saw in her trunk in the Rite-Aid bag and decide to go along with it anyway. "Haven't used it yet," I consent. "Why not?"

"Yeah," she says. "It'll be nice ... Won't it?"

"Sure," I say. "Of course."

4

I DON'T KNOW WHY ALLIE seems to have no friends. She's gorgeous; she grew up here; you'd think everybody would know her. And yet she's a ghost—a mere whisper of a person. "I can be kind of a … *private* … person," she once told me, and that was an understatement if I ever heard one. It was about a month after we first started dating, almost a year ago. School had just started up the week before and I was still getting used to the new routine, when that first Saturday night of the semester Allie came knocking at my door at some obscene hour—3 AM, maybe, possibly even four.

It was the hottest night in recent memory, and Ivan and I were up late together in our room. Our room was small—one of those nondescript dormitory dumps you see on so many college campuses—and our beds were on opposite sides of the room, with only about two feet of spare room between them. I had been on my bed, staring up at the ceiling, talking about life, about Allie, and Ivan was on his own bed, leaning over a game of solitaire he had set up on his desk chair. The heat was stultifying that night. We would've gone out, but outside was no better.

"Maybe I should call Allie," I said, wiping the sweat from my forehead. "You've never met her, have you?"

"I have not," Ivan replied, looking over his cards. "You seem to like her very much," he said, and I told her that I did—that I was crazy about her.

"Why do you like her?" he asked.

"Why do I like her?"

"Yes. You seem to like her very much. Why do you like her?"

"I dunno," I said, shrugging. I took a break from looking up at the ceiling and looked over at Ivan, but he was still transfixed by his game. Somehow, I felt the need to defend myself.

"I think it's better if you can't describe why you like somebody though, because how are you supposed to describe why you like somebody anyway? It's not like I can go down a laundry list, you know?" Ivan didn't reply, but only continued to stare at his cards, scratching at his beard as he did so.

"She's gorgeous though," I said.

"Oh?"

"Yeah. I'm really not just saying that, either, dude. It's nuts. You wouldn't believe it."

"What would I not believe?" he asked absentmindedly, moving one of his cards around.

"You wouldn't believe it. *I* can hardly believe it. Like, girls this hot aren't *supposed* to date me."

"I do not know what you mean," he said, and continued to play his cards.

"She's smart too, man. *Way* smarter than me. I don't know what the hell she's even talking about half the time."

"Why is that a good thing?" he asked, looking up at me.

"What, her being smart?"

"No, the idea that you do not understand her. You say that as if it were good."

"Because it means she's deep, man. It means she's got some *substance* to her."

"I often do not understand you," he said, throwing the cards back together and shuffling them up again, "and I do not mistake this for deepness."

"Depth."

"I am sorry?" he asked, looking up from his cards.

"Depth, man, depth."

"I see," he said, and went about setting up his new game.

It wasn't until later, *much* later, that we heard the knocking at the door — shy at first, confident and restless later. My bed was the closest to the door, but about all I could manage was a toss, a turn and a moan.

Knock knock knock.

"Jesus Christ," I groaned. "What time is it?"

Knock knock knock.
"Go away!"
Knock knock knock.
"Go *away*!"
Ivan turned on the desk lamp by his bed and threw off his sheets.
"Sean, it's me," I heard Allie say, knocking again. "Can you answer the door?"
"Oh, what the hell," I muttered, turning over in my bed, looking at Ivan. Ivan just looked back at me and shrugged.
"Please answer the door," I heard her say. "Please answer..."
I sighed and sat up in my bed. "Just a second," I said, stretching, planting my feet on the linoleum floor. I scratched at my ribs and yawned.
Knock knock knock.
"Will you let her in?" Ivan said, looking at me with a raised eyebrow. "There may be something wrong."
"I'm on it," I said, wiping my eyes. "Everybody should probably calm down."
Knock knock knock.
Ivan sighed and shook his head. "Very well," he said, and then standing up, went for the door and answered it in my stead.
Standing in the open doorway in a sundress, Allie had her arms crossed, her hair a mess, her eyes hiding behind her black sunglasses. "Oh," she said, seeing Ivan.
"Dammit, Ivan." I got up from my bed and went to the door. " —I was on my way. Allie, sorry." Taking a step back into the hallway, Allie still had her arms crossed, looking Ivan up and down.
"I'm sorry," she said, almost motioning to leave. "It's so late..."
" —No, no," I said, sleepily shaking my head. "It's fine, it's fine."
Allie continued to stare at Ivan from behind her sunglasses.
"I am sorry," he said, "we have not met. My name is Ivan." Ivan extended his hand to her.
"Allie," she said, taking it, but the rest of her body held back where her hand didn't.
"I'm sorry," I said, turning to Ivan, " —could you give us a second?" Ivan nodded and walked back into the room, closing the door behind him to leave us out in the hallway.
"Hey," I said, squinting as my eyes adjusted to the pale fluorescent hallway lights. " —is everything okay?"

Allie looked at me uneasily and turned away to look back behind her, over her shoulder — as if someone were watching — as if someone were coming — and then turned back to face me once more.

"Hey," I said, taking her hands as she uncrossed them. "It's okay. I'm here." Allie looked up at me, but her eyes were still hidden by her sunglasses; I let go of her hands to smooth her messy, tangled hair. The blank, black lenses of her sunglasses stared up at me in vacuity. "Come on," I said, resting my hands on her bare shoulders, "everything's okay."

"I'm sorry," she said, slowly coming in closer as I held her in my arms. "It's so late," she said. "It's so late."

"It's okay," I said, holding her to me. Her skin was cool, clammy to the touch. "It's okay."

Allie laughed nervously, her body lurching in awkward spasms. "Figures, the one time I come visit you it's in the middle of the night, right? I even woke up your roommate."

"Hey." I separated from her and kept my hands on her shoulders. "What's wrong?"

Allie looked up at me but could hardly sustain it, even with her sunglasses. She looked down at her feet and said nothing for some time; a fluorescent light flickered noisily from above. She looked so beautiful that night. She was dressed in a sundress, the likes of which I had never seen on her, red and orange and girlish and beautiful. So beautiful. Even with her hair frizzed up in the dampness, her cheeks flushed from the heat. I would've done anything for her that night.

"Would you mind … " she started, still looking downward. "I mean, would it be okay … " She looked up at me uneasily. " — if I spent the night tonight?" I took her by the hand and smiled, and then she smiled too, for the first time all night. "I would like to spend the night tonight."

"Of course," I said, pressing her hand with mine. "Of course you can … Why didn't you just say so before?" Allie didn't respond. "You know you can always come to me — why didn't you just give me a call?" Allie still didn't respond, but moving close to me, she kissed me instead. She smiled, kissed me gently and came in close again for me to hold her in my arms, warmer than before; and holding her there, close to me in the hot, fluorescent hallway, I felt all of my questions evaporate away. And somewhere back in the recesses of my mind, I knew, perhaps, that I should have pressed her more; but I felt like kissing and holding her answered all of my questions.

"Thank you," I heard her whisper, and I kissed the top of her head. "Thank you." When we separated Allie looked down over her dress and laughed. "Look at me. I changed before I got here, and somehow this was the first thing I grabbed. Not pajamas, but a sundress."

"It looks nice."

Allie smiled at me. "Just give me a second," she said, touching me gently. "I'll be right back."

Later, I went back into the room alone, shutting the door behind me and leaving it unlocked for Allie.

"What was wrong?" I heard Ivan ask in the darkness.

"Nothing," I said, crawling into bed. "Allie's going to spend the night. She just went to the bathroom first."

"She is spending the night?"

"Yeah," I said, and neither of us spoke for a minute or more, the silence hanging densely overhead; it was Ivan who finally broke it.

"And why, exactly, did she feel the urge to spend the night when it was already nearly morning?"

"Oh, who cares," I said, turning over to face the wall. "Go to sleep."

"I will," he said, " —if I can."

"What the hell does that mean?" I said, restarting.

"It means I will sleep if neither of you keep me awake."

"Oh, come on," I said, turning back over to face him. "We've barely been together a month, dude. I told you, we've never had sex."

"And I hope it remains that way," he replied. "At least through tonight."

I snickered. "Right," I said. "Thanks, Russki."

"So why did she come this late?" he asked, ignoring me. "Clearly, it was not for you."

I laughed involuntarily. "Dude, really, it's fine."

"So you do not know then."

"She didn't tell me."

"And you do not think this is strange?"

"What's strange," I said, raising my voice, "is the fact that you're so goddamn interested."

"Have it your way," he said, turning away from me to lie on his back. "But it is strange."

Ivan always has to have the last say on things—always has to get in the last provocative word before going silent—and silent things became. Outside the window, I heard the last drunken stragglers trudging their way back to the dorms, most of them quieter than when they first left, others yelling out arbitrary half words at nothing. I lay on my back and stared up at the ceiling, pale blue and luminescent from the full moon in the window. After the drunkards had passed, there was scarcely a sound to be heard. Out in the hall, I heard a door close—probably from the ladies' room—and later, Allie's footsteps approaching.

"She is very beautiful," I heard Ivan say. He rolled over onto his other side and faced the wall away from me. "Very, very beautiful." I looked over at him, at his back facing me, as if he would speak once more, although he never did. Just like Ivan, I figured. Only, this time I didn't mind. This time, I almost kind of liked it.

The door opened, shut quietly again, and then Allie was in the bed next to me, her skin smooth and cool to the touch.

"I'm sorry I'm so cold," she whispered. "I washed up a bit."

"It's okay," I said, giving her a kiss. "It's too hot in here anyway." Allie kissed me back and snuggled up close to me, her front to my back, her arms wrapped around my chest, her breasts cushioning my back.

"You wanna be big spoon, huh?" I said, smiling although she couldn't see it.

"Hmm?"

"Well I don't mind being little spoon every once in a while."

" …What do you mean?"

"Nothing," I said, thinking that maybe in my sleepiness I wasn't making sense. "—just have never spooned with you before, is all."

"Spooned…" I heard her whisper softly behind me. The word sounded unfamiliar to her. I could hear her measuring its meaning in her mind. "I've never spooned with anyone."

" …Are you serious?"

Allie never replied. I could feel her breathing on the back of my neck, but in the heat of the night, I found myself too tired to care.

So I closed my eyes—let the darkness take me as I steadily felt my breathing change—felt the slow, languid dip back into sleep as the first morning birds chirped in isolated half tunes outside my window. It was Allie who shook me out of it—Allie who shook me gently and whispered my name into my ear.

"Sean?" she said. "Sean."

"Yeah," I muttered drowsily. "Yeah, yeah."

I was still facing the wall, but then Allie turned me over with her hands, not moving me but only guiding me gently until we faced one another. It was the first time all night I saw her without her sunglasses, I realized. Her eyes were smaller and frailer than I might have remembered—smaller and frailer than I might have known.

"Sean," she said, looking into my eyes, "I'm sorry about tonight. I'm really, *really* sorry."

"No, no," I said. "I'm glad you came. I'm just sorry I'm not more awake, you know?"

Allie smiled slightly and took me by the hand and held it with both of hers. She brought it to her lips and kissed it tenderly before bringing it down and holding it warm against her chest.

Allie sighed and closed her eyes. "I know ... " she started, but her voice broke off into the silence. She opened her eyes again, looked into me and continued. "I know I can be kind of a ... *private* ... person ... sometimes ... But I'm trying to be better, Sean. I'm really, really trying." Taking the hand she held with hers, I brought her hands to my lips and kissed them, too.

"I understand," I said, but somehow, I didn't. "I do understand."

"Sean?" she said, in just the slightest whisper. "Do you know a Rachel? An Adam?"

"Hmm?" I suddenly felt too tired for this. "I dunno. What're their last names?"

Allie closed her eyes and pressed my hand tightly with hers. "I won't do this again," she said in a murmuring. "I *won't* do this again."

"Hey," I said, "it's not a big deal."

Allie opened her eyes and looked into mine one last time before closing them finally for the night. "It *is* a big deal," she whispered. "I'm sorry."

5

Allie lets me cut the tomatoes, lets me stir the pasta, calls me her "sous chef" and reassures me that we're cooking the meal "together," but even I know better, and it's not long before she shoos me out of the house altogether. "The AC's been on a good hour now," she says. "Would you mind going out back by the river for some firewood?"

When I end up going outside, it's getting a little cooler and the sun's setting down low behind the Mohonk Mountain. The ridge darkens black in the shadows and glows warm pink and purple from behind it. Directly ahead of me, the land descends abruptly for about ten feet before letting off to the banks of the river, moving slowly with a silent ease. Across the river, a road winds off through the low-lying flood plains and eventually makes for the silhouetted Mohonk set back against the horizon. Looking out, I eventually spot Ivan, sitting by the shore on a collapsed tree.

"Hey," I say as I approach him. He turns around to see me before he nods, a quiet little smile playing secretly upon his lips. The tree he's sitting on is clean and picked dry by the sun, its bare branches reaching down to dip their longing fingers in the river below.

"Hello, Sean," he says, and motions for me to sit down next to him, and I do. He looks over at the kindling in my hands.

"Don't ask."

He shrugs. "If you insist," he says, and then we both just stare out at the sunset for some time. The Wallkill River marks the end of town. After that are the flood plains, some farmland, the mountains and then only more mountains again.

"What're you doing out here?" I ask him.

"Hmm?" he muses. "I was just getting a breath of fresh air, actually, when I noticed the sunset." He remains quiet for a few seconds before taking a deep breath. "This place is really … very pretty."

"I know."

He nods very slowly before finally turning to me a bit. "Where are you and Allie going tomorrow?"

"The Catskills," I say, motioning off toward the northwest.

"Oh?"

"Yeah."

"The Catskills are very nice, actually … very … pretty."

"I know. Allie's crazy about them, and we've been meaning to do this for a while now. It's just always been difficult, you know, with school and work and our schedules and all."

Ivan nods silently and looks back out at the sunset. "And you will be hiking the whole weekend?"

"Yeah," I reply. "It's this trail called 'devil's path.'" Ivan looks at me with a raised eyebrow. "I know. The name kinda sums it up, from what I hear. 'Twenty-something miles of some of the toughest hiking in the whole northeast,' from what Allie's told me."

"Is that right?"

"Yeah, well, Allie's not the kinda girl who'd want to go out to some restaurant, and I've got enough restaurant in me to last a lifetime." Ivan says nothing so I just keep going. "It's kinda how we got together though, you know? Hiking and nature and stuff. It kinda makes sense for us to do this sorta thing for our anniversary."

I wait for a reply but never get one. Ivan is looking out, enjoying the sunset, I suppose, but when I look over at him I see that he's got his eyes closed, his hands folded in his lap. His eyelids flicker momentarily. A fly buzzes defiantly and approaches from the river; it hovers about him awkwardly, but Ivan remains still. The fly buzzes back toward the river again, but his eyes remain closed; his eyes remain still. A frown deepens upon his face, furrows intimately about his eyebrows before disappearing entirely; and when he opens up his eyes, Ivan merely smiles at me, rising up from the log as if in ascension.

"Do have a good time, Sean," he says, and he starts making his way back to the house. "I will be here when you return."

I turn to watch him go, to watch his back as he walks away to leave me alone on the tree, collapsed and sleeping half in the mud, half in the river beside me. Ivan walks slowly back up toward the rail trail, toward our house on the other side, and passes briefly beneath a willow before turning back to look to me. I almost think of saying something, some goodbye, some something of what, I don't know, but then he turns away and makes for the house once more. I turn then too, look back out at the blackened ridge, at the sky swallowing it up into its darkening, purple darkness. The sun is setting truly now; the sun will soon be gone.

Time to get the firewood. Time to get the fire good and going.

6

T HE NEXT MORNING AFTER Allie stayed over that first time, I woke up to the sun shining in my eyes. I woke up almost spasmodically, lurching out of my bed all at once. Allie roused in the bed next to me.

"Mmmm," she hummed, and wiped at her eyes. "Is something wrong?"

"No," I said, looking around the room. Ivan's bed was empty. The room was clean, cool, and bright from the sun in the window. Everything was fine—but my heart was pounding. "I think I just had a dream," I said, and slowly lay back down, my heart still pumping hard in my chest.

Allie rolled over onto her side to face me, looking dreamily into my eyes. "What were you dreaming about?"

I scoured my mind in a panic. "I…don't remember," I said, and somehow, I was troubled. "—why can't I remember?"

"I never remember my dreams," she said, smiling, and then lay back over on her back, stretching her arms up to the ceiling. Allie hummed lightly, like music. "You know," she said, "I kinda like waking up next to you."

But I was somewhere else. Lying there, on my back, staring at the ceiling, all I could do was think, trying desperately to summon the memories of my dream back to my conscious mind, always failing, always slipping away from me like oil in my hands. What was it? And why could I not remember? My heart gradually began to slow its way back down to a normal, reasonable pace.

"What happened to you last night?" I asked, still looking up at the ceiling.

Allie paused before replying, a caesura that rang abruptly in my ears. "What happened to me?" she asked, as if not knowing what I could possibly mean.

"Well something must have happened, right? You came by in the middle of the night and looked like you had just seen a ghost."

"A ghost..." Allie whispered. I rolled over onto my side to face her, but now Allie was looking down at the sheets, away from me. "It's hard to explain," she said, looking up at me shyly.

"What's hard to explain?"

"It's just...very hard to explain."

"Well, what's wrong?"

Allie sighed and stayed silent for several seconds more. "Do you trust me, Sean?"

"Do I trust you?"

"Yes. Do you trust me?"

"...Sure I trust you," I said, but I had to stop and think about it first.

"It'd just be...very hard for you to understand."

"What'd be so hard for me to understand?"

Allie looked at me with a sadness I didn't expect, somehow, and looked away one last time. "Everything," she said, and then covered her face with her hands. "Everything," she said, and I think I heard her cry. "Everything."

7

"Do you love me, Sean?"

"What?"

"I said, do you love me?"

I try to look Allie in the eyes but end up laughing involuntarily instead; Allie laughs too, the seriousness in her face breaking as she waves about her hand to silence us both. She takes a moment to collect her thoughts, the fire crackling in the background, the air conditioner roaring out behind her as well.

"Seriously," she says. "I'm serious, I mean it. I mean … do you *really* love me?" Her small green eyes dance frailly in the firelight.

"Of course I love you." Allie looks straight into me in what would be the silence were it not for the contradicting counterpoint of the fireplace and the air conditioner, and eventually betrays a grin; Allie points at me playfully.

"I don't believe you," she says, her finger dangling before my eyes. "I don't believe you because I love you *so* much, Sean, and I *know* you don't feel the same way *I* do." I take her hand and kiss it a few times. My kisses get inevitably wetter as they go along, and I begin to reel her in by the arm when she laughs and stops me gently.

"Stop," she says, laughing still. She takes a sip from her jack-and-coke with her free hand and puts the hand I just kissed on my cheek. "Think you can change the subject?" she asks, smiling. "You can't fool me," she sing-songs lightly. "You can't fool me."

After that we're both quiet for some time as we look at each other in the trembling light, her hand never leaving my cheek. I try not to, but eventually I crack a smile.

"What?" she giggles.

"You're really different," I say, leaning away from her on my pillows.

"Different like what?" Allie finishes the jack-and-coke and looks around before finding a half-drunk glass of wine on the nightstand. She takes only a small sip before letting it rest in her lap.

"You're a different drunk than I remember." She cocks her head at me. "Not that I have much of a frame of reference."

"Oh … You mean the night we met."

I nod and take a sip from my own jack-and-coke before placing it back on the nightstand. Allie's looking down at her hands as they play idly with her wineglass.

"Why do you say that?" she asks, quieter than I'd expect.

"I dunno … No reason, really. Just a thought."

"But where'd the thought come from?" Allie's eyes never leave her glass or her hands as they play with it; she says nothing, and then I hear her murmur something softly in the silence.

"What?" I ask. "What'd you say?"

"I said talking in bed ought to be easiest." Her eyes come up from her wineglass and set themselves upon me. I have to struggle to answer her.

"Well … You were just, so … you know … outgoing and happy-go-lucky and, I dunno … *chatty* the night we met."

She looks off somewhere, away from me. "Was I?"

"Yeah. I never see you like that. You're always kind of in your own world, you know? Even now." Allie looks back up at me. "Like, I don't know what you're thinking now. You could be thinking anything. But that first night you weren't like that." She's playing with the drink in her hands. "Until I mentioned Lily, actually. Then you suddenly changed."

Allie looks up at me again and this time she cracks a grin. "Maybe I just liked you," she says, brushing a finger along my chest. "Did you ever think of that?"

"Not really," I say, laughing. "Like I said, I never know *what* you're thinking."

Allie plays with her drink again, but just for a moment this time. "I know," she says. And then she puts her drink down next to her and leans in and hugs me, lies against me with my back to the pillows.

She pets my hair and whispers in my ear: "I'm sorry." She's quiet for some time, until she repeats herself. "I'm sorry. I'm so, so sorry…"

"Hey," I say, moving my hands through her hair too. "It's okay… Everything's okay." Allie pulls away from me and looks into my eyes.

"Do you love me?"

"I love you," I say. "I do."

And then we kiss. Allie brings her right hand to my cheek, her left to the back of my neck, and then she becomes stronger, her tongue searching out for mine, my hands searching out for her, finding her in the contours of her body, in the curves of her hips, the small of her back, the smooth skin going up to her shoulder, to her neck, and then my lips find her there too. And then suddenly she's not on top of me anymore, and it's the other way around, and I'm kissing her madly, holding her hand outstretched, her arm off and away from her body, and I'm kissing her neck and I can feel her heart beating in her chest, can feel her heavy breathing as she gently moans into my ear, and her legs are straddling me, wrapping me in and holding me tight with her thighs when suddenly her hand lets go of mine and knocks over her glass of wine.

"Oh!" she cries, jumping up. Wine stains my white sheets scarlet, seeps into them and runs rivulets along their fibers. "Oh God!" Allie cries, patting at the sheets pointlessly with her bare hands. She looks all about her in desperation, looks for something to clean the stain with but can't find a thing. "Do you have paper towels?" she asks me, getting up in a rush. "There have to be paper towels!"

"Allie, don't worry about it!" I tell her, still laying back in the bed. "It's fine."

Allie stands in the middle of my room and spins around in stupefying circles. "Oh God," she keeps repeating. "Oh God."

"Allie!" I say, getting up myself and taking her hands with mine. "—it's *fine*!" I hold her still with both of my hands before she finally settles and calms down—before I can finally rest my hands on her and bring her close to me again with ease.

"Don't worry about it," I whisper into her ear. "I don't even care. They're just sheets." I feel Allie's heartbeat close to my chest, can feel her heartbeat slow down and relax. "They're just sheets," I repeat to her. "They're just sheets." Together we sit back down on the bed, and only then does Allie laugh, nervously.

"God," she says, "I'm really not used to alcohol, am I?"

I smirk. "Can't ever remember you drinking before."

Allie laughs again and finally seems to relax, the tension loosening from her shoulders as she allows herself to let go of what was never a big deal to begin with. She looks up at me knowingly and smiles secretly in the darkness. "I'm sorry ... I don't know what came over me." She looks at the fire and takes a deep breath through her mouth to regain her footing. "I guess I should probably take it easy with this stuff," she says, motioning over to the last surviving glass of wine, "shouldn't I?"

"Kind of reminds me of the night we first met," I say, moving in closer as I smile.

Allie smirks. "Feeling romantic?"

And then I move in closer. "Maybe," I say, and then we kiss. Allie's hand is on my knee, and it moves steadily to my thigh, and when my hand goes to her waist there's nothing left to hold us back but our clothes, clothes that cast stark shadows and demand barriers. Allie falls to her back on the mattress and I move in on top of her, my hands moving, ever moving, ever seeking to fixate her, to formulate her within my grasp, her body swallowing me like a mirage. And out of that darkness I hear her calling me, calling me to her—and the words I recognize dimly as my name.

"Sean ... " That's me. "Sean ... " That's who I am.

"Sean," she says. "Sean."

Sean, she says, but in the heat of the fire, the cold of the fan in the window, the murkiness of the mattress and the sheer miracle of her body, the lines begin to blur: the lines between thee and me; between thine and mine, until there is only "I"—and she's calling to me.

"Sean ... "

"Sean!"

"Sean, stop!"

And when I come to, I realize just how far I've gone. I grin. Even in spite of everything, I can't help but grin.

I'm sorry, I say. *I'm just wasted. I lost my head.*

It's okay, she says. *I'm drunk too.*

But then I think back and I remember—remember her car, remember the white plastic bag from Rite-Aid and what she left in there, and I can't help but push it one step further. Haven't we forgotten something? She feigns ignorance. Forgotten something in the car?

Forgotten something in the trunk of the car? You tried to hide it from me but I found it. *I found it.* Found the Trojan horseman on his consummating stallion.

And then she pushes me away and looks at me with wide, frightened eyes.

"You found that?" she asks.

"Well, yeah," I say, and my nervous laugh betrays what I realize is already backfiring on me.

And as she stares at me silently in the dim, heated light, I see her pupils trembling. Allie turns away from me; she can't even bear to look me in the eye.

"That was not for you to find."

8

Fog on a river
is a cliché image
of a beautiful thing
I wish I could see:
seen only as a symbol
of itself—an image
that doesn't
actually
exist.

Allie's an English major, and sometimes literature is all she ever seems to think about. She's always reciting poetry, even in the middle of talking to me; the funny part is, sometimes I don't even know the words coming out of her mouth are recitations until she tells me so afterward. "I feed on the specters in books," she once told me, and so she does. But when Allie *reads* poetry—when she reads it and recites it for real—it's like something unholy—an invocation to unknown, heathen gods.

I will arise and go now, and go to Innisfree,
And a small cabin build there, of clay and wattles made;
Nine bean rows will I have there, a hive for the honey-bee,
And live alone in the bee-loud glade.

It was a long time ago that Allie first recited that poem for me. A month after we first started dating? Maybe more? All I know is that it was after the night she came to my room; that had to come first, and everything else came after. But I do remember that first recitation. Allie spoke the poem like a hymn, and when she put the book down her eyes rolled back and her eyelids fluttered. Then she grew silent and breathed—breathed. It reminded me of the Shiva statue in the restaurant.

When she was done, Allie opened up her eyes again and told me that the poem was by a man named Yeats.

"Yeats," I said, remembering a reference to him in a Stephen King book I once read. "I know him." I thought back and struggled to extract the words from my memory, thinking that maybe it'd impress her. "Things fall apart, right? The center cannot hold?"

But Allie only smiled faintly. "There is no center anymore." Then she just kinda looked away and muttered, almost to herself, "And what rough beast, its hour come round at last, slouches towards Bethlehem to be born?" The literary type. I wonder what she'd think of *Death in Venice*, but knowing her, she's probably read it already. Maybe she can explain to me who the hell Phaedrus is.

The first two or three months we were together Allie got me to read all sorts of stuff, and not just poetry either—Anais Nin, Hesse, Kafka and Dostoevsky, among others. At first I just pretended to enjoy the books she lent me. Is this how smart people felt like? I wondered. It kinda felt good. If I practiced, maybe I'd be able to quote random bits of poetry, too. Maybe even *other* people would mistake me for smart. But then Allie would actually try *talking* to me about Steppenwolf this and Underground Man that, and my dreams of literary pretentiousness went down the drain as I learned to re-embrace my stupidity.

"Dear parents, I have always loved you, all the same," Allie said, reading from Kafka.

"What the hell is wrong with this guy," I said in an unguarded moment. "What the hell is his deal, and what the hell is up with his dad?"

After that, things went from bad to worse when Allie decided it was time for me to tackle the so-called "classics" of Greek tragedy. First, Allie took me through Plato, explaining to me that to the Greeks (also pedophiles, apparently, like little Tadzio's beloved Aschenbach), that which was absolutely beautiful was also absolutely true and good. "*Kalon*," she called it, "the Platonic notion that holds all classical works together."

"What about then, you know, stuff like the Holocaust?"

" …What?"

"Well that was true, right? How was that 'good' or 'beautiful'?"

"Not *relative* truth, Sean, *absolute* truth—there's a difference."

"But you told me when we were reading Kafka that truth's a point of view."

"Not for the Greeks it isn't!"

The first "classic" she made me read was the *Medea*, probably the most messed up, twisted play I had yet to have read—a play that basically revolved around a mother's insane quest for revenge being fulfilled by ruthlessly murdering all her own children. Where the so-called *kalon* was in that, I'm sure I don't know, but then Allie made me read that deranged play, the *Agamemnon*, which was even worse. After that was the infamous *Bacchae*, and that, finally, was the last straw. God knows what the hell the *Bacchae* was about. God knows what the hell was wrong with the freakin' Greeks in general. Everything else up to that point I could withstand, even the Dostoevsky and the Nin, but the *Bacchae*—well, that finally took the cake.

"I just don't get it," I said. "So there's this guy, Pentheus, and he's the ruler of this city … "

" —*walled* city."

"Right. So he's the ruler of this walled city, and then this god Dionysus shows up and makes all the women go insane … "

" —the *maenads*," Allie attempted to explain. "Dionysus was the god of wine, of mask, theater and intoxication. He is *Eleutherios*, the liberator who frees people through madness and ecstasy; *Bromios*, the roaring one; the Stranger—he's meant to represent the irrational."

"And he has a group of women called *maenads* who abandon their lives to go live on the mountain with him, where they all get drunk and run around going insane?"

"They were part of the mystery cults."

"What's that?"

"Mystery comes from the word *musterion*."

"That doesn't mean anything to me."

"*Musterion* or mystery is the Greek word for a secret rite. Nobody knew what the mystery rites were except for the initiates, the *mystes*, coming from the words 'closed' or 'shut.' Only those who were initiated into those rites understood the truth of the mysteries; to outsiders, they just looked insane, singing and dancing, naked and drunk — but to the insiders, the initiates, the *mystes*, the *mystics* — the mysteries were Truth. Worshipers of Dionysus were often part of these mystery cults that the play is referencing."

"Cult as in a scientology kind of cult?"

"No, Sean, listen ... "

" — is that why these *maenad* cultists go around tearing peoples' heads off?"

"Listen, you're missing the point ... "

" — I don't think there is a point."

"The *Bacchae* is about the necessity of embracing the irrational, about the necessity of making room for darkness in one's individual and collective life. If you try to deny it or suppress it, it destroys you."

"So you're telling me that Pentheus, the poor leader of this city who has to watch as all the women go insane and join this crazy wine god on the mountain, dancing and singing and getting drunk and running naked, gets torn limb from limb by his own mother, just because he tried to suppress and deny his own dark side?"

"Something like that. His being torn apart is symbolic."

"Allie ... "

"What?"

"That's retarded."

I can't say she was particularly pleased by that one, but on the bright side, Allie mostly left me alone and stopped giving me books to read. I can't really say I blame her, but honestly, I felt bad. I knew how badly she wanted me to love those books the same way she did; I could see she wanted to share her love of literature with me the same way she had shared her love for mountains and waterfalls — our relationship was first kindled in the partaking of that love. But I dunno, I've always loved nature; I've always loved mountains. Hiking and exploring was stuff I could wrap my head around. All that poetry, all that Kafkaesque nonsense — it was all just too abstract, too foreign to me. It became like some kind of exotic realm for me, some separate world of aesthetics and form that I could never penetrate, never understand. There was something mystical about it, even, something secret — as if Allie were initiated in its rites and mysteries and I was not. I tried; and perhaps the fact that I tried and failed was what got to Allie the most. She was one of the mystic initiates; and I was just an ignorant outsider.

But it was hard for me too, and that, perhaps, is what I never told her. Did she think I liked feeling stupid? That I wore it as a point of pride? I had never thought of myself as a stupid person before, or at least not until I met Allie. Sure, maybe I wasn't the smartest guy in the world, but I got by; I made it to a good college, studied hard and made my grades, and that was something to be proud of too, wasn't it? Just because I can't decode the secret significance of pedophilia and its relation to the "amorality of aesthetics" in a book like *Death in Venice* doesn't make me stupid — it's just hard for me to understand things I can't hold in my hands or feel for myself. I know the meanings of words, and even know how to use them well — it's when they're strung together into symbolic abstractions that seem to have no connection to reality that I begin to get confused.

None of this was good enough for Allie, of course, and so finally one time she sat me down and really tried to get me to understand. She brought me all the way out into the woods, I remember, the middle of nowhere and made me sit down on this log while I listened to her recite this poem, "The Lady of Shalott," by Alfred Tennyson; a poem that, according to Allie, was about a woman cursed to live in a tower, weaving pictures of the world through a mirror, never allowed to look upon reality with her own two eyes. Allie sat across from me on another log and had me sit still and silent for something like thirty seconds before she even started; and when she did start, it was like a conjuring — like pagan witchcraft — her voice intoning and inflecting while her arms waved wildly about in the sacred summoning of the poem's power:

> There she weaves by night and day
> A magic web with colors gay.
> She has heard a whisper say,
> *A curse is on her if she stay*
> To look down to Camelot.
>
> She knows not what the curse may be,
> And so she weaveth steadily,
> And little other care hath she,
> The Lady of Shalott.

And moving through a mirror clear
That hangs before her all the year,
Shadows of the world appear.
There she sees the highway near
Winding down to Camelot.
There the river eddy whirls,
And there the surly village churls,
And the red cloaks of market girls,
Pass onward from Shalott.

Sometimes a troop of damsels glad,
An abbot on an ambling pad,
Sometimes a curly shepherd lad,
Or long-haired page in crimson clad,
Goes by to towered Camelot;
And sometimes through the mirror blue
The knights come riding two and two:
She hath no loyal knight and true,
The Lady of Shalott.

But in her web she still delights
To weave the mirror's magic sights;
For often through the silent nights
A funeral, with plumes and lights
And music, went to Camelot.
Or when the moon was overhead,
Came two young lovers lately wed:
"I am half sick of shadows," said
The Lady of Shalott.

The poem went on like that; eventually the Lady of Shalott couldn't
help but look down on the real world when Lancelot went by. After
that, the mirror she used to look upon the world cracked in half and
she left the tower; then for another reason that I didn't really understand, she sang one last song and died.

When Allie was finished, it was like a temple after prayer. Her voice
let off to the wind in the trees and I could hear the crickets and the
June bugs and the water in the rocks; it was like someone charged
the air with an electric current, and you could hear it humming. But

when she opened up her eyes again, they were looking at me. I looked back at them for a moment too, but I couldn't sustain it; I looked away. After that I just rocked a little on the log, back and forth, trying to pretend everything was okay. "You're really good at reciting poetry," I said, my eyes diffidently venturing to meet hers. Then it was Allie's turn to look away.

"Come on," she said, standing up, "we better head back."

She wasn't herself the rest of the walk back—she didn't even bother to tell me about the woods we were walking through; we could've been anywhere. I tried wheedling it out of her, but it was no use—I felt like I was talking to her from behind a veil. And I don't even know what the hell I was supposed to feel sorry for, but somehow, I was—I was really, really sorry, and I would've done anything in the world to have let her know. Instead, I walked lamely and stared at my feet most of the way back.

I got to thinking a lot about Lily during that walk. I hadn't thought about her in a long time, but I was thinking about her then. I thought about the time I told her I loved her. I really did love her—I loved her the first night we ever met, and I wanted to tell her for so long, but I knew it would ruin things. I *knew* it would ruin everything, and every night I spent with her I had to close my eyes and wish the words away, banish them into silence where I thought they would do no harm. The night I eventually did tell her we had just finished making love. Lily was staring up at me, gently moving her hands through my hair and I was just laying there, holding her, looking into her eyes. And I was so drunk that night—so very drunk. I couldn't help what I said. We were lying in each other's sweat. I couldn't help it. The words came out of their own accord, and the silence that ensued told me all the rest. All was over, all was done. The gig was up. Lily just laughed eventually, like she always did. *Well,* her laugh said, *that was fun, wasn't it?*

I looked up from my feet and watched Allie's back as she moved—watched her hair bob with her gait, her hips sway at the rocking of her walk. Well, that was fun while it lasted, too. But I always knew this time was coming. How did I ever end up with a girl like Allie, anyway—a girl far better looking and smarter than me? How could something like that ever possibly last? I was constantly waiting for the axe to fall, because something that good could've only happened to me by mistake. Being with Allie I was a liar, a cheat, a fraud and a fake, and the whole world knew it. I guess it was only a matter of time before Allie woke up to the truth too.

…I don't really remember much of the walk back. I don't remember much of the drive back…but later on, at the end of it all, when Allie pulled up to the curb in front of my dorm, all I could hear was the idling of her engine and all I could feel was the sinking in my stomach. Allie was tapping her fingers impatiently at the wheel, not even bothering to shift the car into park. Sitting there in my seat, I did little more than stare at my shoes, but somehow, I wasn't moving; the gig was up, just like last time — but somehow, I couldn't just leave. I couldn't bring myself to just get up and go. As cowardly as I am.

"Listen," I finally said, "is everything…okay?" Dead silence. Allie was wearing sunglasses and she was still facing forward — her hands at ten-and-two, her foot pressed to the brake, waiting and ready to run off the moment I left… *But I still couldn't just leave.*

"Is there anything…anything that I can…that I can *do*?"

There was silence for a long time. I heard her sigh in that silence — saw her lean forward slowly and nearly press her forehead to the wheel. I steeled my nerves and awaited the inevitable — waited for the "listen…" the "we need to talk," or, even worse, the "there's nothing to talk about."

But something happened that day — a *miracle* that happened that day — and the last thing I expected to see, I saw — *her smile*. She smiled behind those sunglasses, and even with her face leaning forward into the steering wheel, she couldn't hide it from me. And when she did turn to me, her smile was so *there*, so undeniably *there* — that smile that she kept only for me — she smiled and she took my hand and massaged it with hers. So warm, I remember. Like an electric blanket.

"I love you," she said. "I do." And then she kissed me — as if it were the very first time.

When I got out of the car I felt dizzy, felt confused, felt completely unsure of anything that had just happened. My hands and arms were buzzing — tingling and nervous — my heart was beating hard. I massaged my chest with my hands, still warm from hers, and watched as she drove away, the wind enveloping me before carrying on. I stood there and kept massaging, feeling the heart inside of me — feeling its pumping inside my ribcage — feeling its mortal reality beneath my skin and bones; and such a wave of feelings rose up inside of me all at once that I nearly cried — like a glass that had been poured too full. I stood there and couldn't speak, couldn't see — deaf and dumb and blind and blushing — and to this day I don't know why.

"Oh God," I heard myself saying as I clutched my chest. "God, oh God, oh God, oh God." Like some kind of holy, mantric chant.

When I walked into my room a few minutes later, my phone was ringing. It was Allie, calling just to say hi. As if the whole past few hours had never even happened. As if it had all just been a bad dream. And I never would've dared to, but I wanted to tell her that I missed her — that I missed her dearly and would've done anything in the world to have her by my side at that moment, in my arms, if only to validate her existence. "Are you real?" I wanted to ask her. "Are you really, *really* real?"

*　*　*　*　*

That was the first time Allie ever told me she loved me, and I wish I could say that it all ended there — that Allie said it and so, she meant it, and with it came the whole package: love, intimacy, sex and commitment. But it all takes time. With Allie, everything does. By that point we had already been dating for some months, and I still hadn't even seen her place. As if I had passed some test, Allie didn't bring me over there until the day after she first told me she loved me: to Lenape Hall, set close to the woods that separate campus from town.

Allie didn't open the door for me when I first knocked. I knocked again.

"Come in," I heard her say. Opening the door, I saw Allie sprawled out on her bed, her head buried in some book that looked about as thick as my thigh. Walking inside and moving closer, I made out "Leo Tolstoy" on the binding and almost had the bad sense to ask her what it was; remembering what had happened the day before, I thought the better of it.

Consumed by her book, Allie didn't even acknowledge me at first. I thought of maybe clearing my throat, if only to announce my presence, but decided she probably wouldn't hear me over the music blaring out of the speakers set on the bookcase. Ridiculous music. *Romantic music* — it was hard to believe — so romantic, it sounded like a parody of itself. It sounded oddly familiar too. I vaguely remembered seeing it in some black-and-white movie, possibly, or maybe even in an old Bugs Bunny cartoon. "What's that?" I asked. "Mozart?"

Allie turned and looked up at me standing there before her but didn't move. She half smiled and closed the book with a loud thud and tossed it carelessly back on her shelf. "Rachmaninoff," she said. "His second piano concerto."

"Ah," I said, recognizing the name from the Willy Wonka movie. "Rachmaninoff."

"Come over here," Allie said, motioning with her hand. "Come sit next to me. I missed you."

Sitting down next to her on the bed, I had the uncanny feeling that I was in a bizarre, foreign place, and one in which I did not belong. There was that absurd music playing, books *everywhere,* strewn all over the floor, across her desk—I even found a copy of *Heart of Darkness* underneath her pillow. It looked like something out of a movie—like a caricature of a room, and not close to being the real thing.

The books weren't the end of it, either; all over her walls were art prints, big and small. Some of the stuff I kind of knew—Van Gogh I can recognize, but a good deal of the rest of it was more obscure, at least for a dope like me. There was one in particular that caught my eye: a painting of a beautiful, brown-haired girl, dead and drowned in this little measly stream. The girl looked really surprised, actually. Like she couldn't believe she had just drowned in such a measly little stream. There were flowers in her hands.

"What's that painting?" I asked.

"That's Ophelia," Allie said, looking up at it, "from *Hamlet.*"

"Ohhh," I said. For once I actually *got* the reference. I had to read *Hamlet* in my senior year of high school; Ophelia, I recalled, was the girl who lost her mind and was later found dead in the river.

"So…why do you have a painting of her, dead, on the wall?" And then I was surprised to hear it myself, but I heard Allie giggle—just a little snort of it—but a giggle nonetheless. I turned away from the painting on the wall and saw her to already be looking right into me, a smirk playing upon her lips.

"Did I say something?"

I couldn't believe the look she was giving me then, her face so close to mine. Her lips twisted into an unconscious simper, her eyes narrowed and staring, I almost felt the urge to back away from her. It was crude—unnatural, even. It was a look of hunger; it was a look of desire. But put on, somehow—affected—as ridiculous as the music playing on in the background—as the books stashed beneath her pillows.

"Hi," she said.

"Hey."

I'm not really sure what happened next. She was sitting next to me one second and was on top of me the next—kissing me, pinning me down to the bed, tearing off my clothes, biting at my neck—I had no idea what was even going on. I had never seen that side of her before, and gladly. I wasn't prepared for it, nor did I have any part in what was going on—she stripped herself down without any help from me, and before I even knew what was what, she had stopped—stopped abruptly with her on top of me, her bare breasts pushing into my chest, her small hands grappling my cheeks, her trembling eyes anchored directly upon mine.

"Allie?" I looked up and down at her nearly naked body, her small black panties the only item left. "Allie, what is it?"

Allie said nothing but only kept on breathing, her eyes never leaving mine. She kept looking at me, into my eyes, but I kept looking down at her body, taking it in for the first time, my eyes doing laps up and down and around her tremendous, delicate curves. I'd make eye contact, look down at her again, make eye contact, look down at her again, and all the while Allie's eyes had still never left mine.

"Oh God," she said, still staring into me. Her hands began to loosen their grip from my head. "Oh God." And for the briefest of moments, I saw her eyes glaze over—a thin gloss before she finally looked away and laid her head softly on my chest.

I lay there, saying nothing for what must've been a minute, and tried to figure out what the hell had just happened and what, if anything, I was supposed to do about it. I put my hands in her hair and gently massaged her scalp; I looked down the length of the back of her body, at what only her black little panties could still tease away. Good God, I thought. What, exactly, was expected of me?

"Listen," I said at last, "we don't *have* to do this ... if you don't want to ... "

I didn't even quite understand what it was I proposing to postpone, but I felt her breathe deeply and sigh. She replied to me in just a whisper, just into my ear: "If I were not myself ... If I were free ... "

" ...Okay."

"Tolstoy," she said, smiling with effort. "Isn't it beautiful?"

I didn't know what to think then, but I do now. It's an utter crock of shit. Who cares if something's beautiful if it's still pure bullshit? Kalon, my ass. Fuck Tolstoy and fuck poetry. What, exactly, is the point of art if all it does is keep people like Allie from dealing with real life? What the hell is it with me and relationships, anyway? With Lily sex was fair game and love—well, love was just too real. With Allie, apparently, it was the other way around. "If I were not myself," she had said. "If I were free." Fine. Sure. Whatever. Only, who exactly would she rather be, if not herself, and what is she trying to free herself from?

The rest of the scene was anti-climactic, at least for me. Allie gave me a perfunctory peck on the forehead and put her clothes back on, and I had no choice left but to do the same. I shoved on my pants, got myself back into my tee-shirt, and then just sat there, left to wonder what the hell had just happened to me. I watched Allie's bare back from the other side of the bed. Watched as she managed to fit herself back into her jeans; as she clipped closed the back of her bra. Well, I thought. There goes that.

"Hey, Sean?"

"Yeah?" I asked with reluctance. She was just finally getting her halter top back on.

"Do you want to take dancing lessons with me?"

" ... I'm sorry, what?"

"Waltzing lessons, I mean."

" ...Waltzing lessons."

"Yeah. Waltzing lessons."

" ...Are you serious?"

"Do you want to dance with me?" she snapped, suddenly turning to glare at me, "or don't you?"

I did. More than anything, I did. "Yes," I said, because deep down inside, I'm even more cowardly than I give myself credit for.

*   *   *   *   *

I whispered: "Where do I put my hands again?"

But Allie just smiled and guided my left hand to join with her right—guided my right hand to cradle her back so I could lead her from behind. Standing there awkwardly in the dance studio, trying my best to look like I belonged there among the other couples, Allie laughed at me with her eyes until the music began.

"One-two-three," the woman leading the class repeated over the lazy din of the stereo.

"One-two-three," she said. "One-two-three."

Allie and I, meanwhile, tripped over each other's feet, stumbling as we held each other up. Allie laughed and then I couldn't help but laugh, too. How often do I get to see Allie laugh? I was happy to be there.

Allie exaggerated her posture and primped up her face. "Look the part," she said, turning with me in a graceful flourish.

"You mean become a human clothes hanger?"

Allie laughed. "It's half the battle."

"One-two-three," the woman droned in the background, walking between the couples. "One-two-three."

"How do I like, spin you or whatever?"

Allie guided me with her hands more than I was guiding her. "This is waltzing," she said.

"Meaning?"

"Meaning you don't signal — you choreograph."

"Well okay then. This is me choreographing you, so get yourself ready."

Allie laughed. "You gonna strut your stuff?"

"Better believe it," I said, and spun her so messily, we nearly bumped into the couple next to us.

"That was impressive," Allie said, smiling as the couple left us.

"I have my moments."

The woman leading the class stood next to us and watched us as we turned. "Tippy toes," she said to me. "Always remember to stay on your tippy toes."

"One-two-three," she echoed, walking away. "One-two-three."

"This is ridiculous," I said as she left our earshot.

"Just admit it."

"Admit what?"

Allie smirked. "That you love it."

"I love *you*," I said, saying the words she had only said to me a few days before. "Dancing, maybe."

"Very good," the woman called over us, turning off the music. "Now, let us try something a tiny bit more difficult."

"I love you too," Allie said, looking down at the floor, nearly whispering.

"I'm sorry, what?"

Allie looked up at me with small, trembling eyes. "I said I love you."

"Tales from Vienna Woods," the woman said, putting a CD in her stereo, "by Johann Strauss, Jr."

A flute interlude came out from the speakers. I stood as straight as I could, and held out my arms in the proper, mechanical posture. Allie was looking away from me. The woman leading the class started moving her arms to a rhythm. "Aaaand…" she intoned, and suddenly horns kicked in. "One-two-three," she said, signaling us to start. "One-two-three."

"Hey," I said, squeezing Allie's hand, "are you okay?"

Allie looked up at me and smiled, sadly. "Yes. Yes, of course."

"Come on," I said, smiling back at her. "Dance like you mean it."

Allie's eyes held mine. "Like I love it?" she ventured, and I didn't back away.

"Exactly."

"Are you listening to that rhythm?" the woman leading the class asked the room. "Listen to that rhythm. Listen to that beat. Hear it in your mind: one-two-three; one-two-three. The Hindus have a saying: if something happens once, it may never happen again; but if it happens twice, you can believe by the will of God it will happen again. Dance, now; dance. One-two-three. One-two-three."

"Tell me a story," Allie said, coming closer to me; closer than waltzing usually affords you.

"A story?"

"Tell me anything," she said, and did away with the posture and rested her head on my shoulder.

"Listen to it," the woman intoned. "Listen. One-two-three. One-two-three."

"We're not in a dance studio," I said, resting my chin atop Allie's head, turning with her in spinning, elongated circles. "We're not here at all."

"Where are we?" she whispered.

"A palace," I said, " —in Vienna. We're in a Viennese palace, and we're not here at all."

Allie hummed quietly in appreciation. "Gilded ceilings? Columned walls?"

"Polished ballroom floors. You can see your own reflection."

"Who else is with us?"

"Only the best. A full orchestra on the sidelines: violins, horns—they surround us with their sound. The royalty are here. The important."

"The beautiful."

"The beautiful," I repeated. "Only the beautiful."

"One-two-three," the woman chanted. "One-two-three."

"What am I wearing?" Allie asked.

"A long white gown."

"A diamond tiara?"

"Long white gloves; they reach up to your elbows."

"And you, with mirror-polished shoes …"

"—with coattails trailing down my backside."

"A true suitor of old?"

"A gentleman for the ages."

"And we're in love," she says, quieter than ever before. "Aren't we?"

"One-two-three!" the woman bellowed louder. "Faster! Faster! One-two-three! One-two-three!"

"Allie?" I asked, but got no reply. "Allie, what's wrong?"

"God," she said, and sobbed tears into my shoulder. "God, oh God, oh God, oh God."

9

"Wait," I say, trying to ignore the drunken buzzing in my brain. "I don't understand."

Allie's still looking down at the stupid drink she's been holding for the past five minutes, not saying a damn thing.

"What do you mean they 'weren't for me to find?'"

"I don't know," she says, almost to herself. "That's what I said, wasn't it?" Allie carelessly tosses the rest of her drink in the fire. It hisses, briefly, then returns to plain silence.

"Well then who, exactly, was supposed to find them?"

Allie looks up at me coldly in the darkening light, daring me to go further. "Is that what you think?"

"What...? No. No, no, of course not. Just...call me crazy, Allie, but I don't understand why somebody would have condoms if they didn't intend on using them."

Allie audibly sighs and rubs at her temples. "Ugh," she groans, "I shouldn't be drunk for this. I shouldn't be drunk. I never should've drank at all."

"Listen," I say, "forget about it. Really. It's not a big deal, all right? I don't care about sex. Not really, anyway. And I know how you feel about sex too...that's why I'm so confused..." She remains non-responsive. "Were you thinking about it or something? Should I not've brought it up? Should I've waited for you?"

"Was I thinking about what?" she asks, and looks at me sideways.

"I dunno...sex?"

"So you want to talk about the thing itself then?"

"Do I want to … ?"

" — why is everything *always* about sex?"

"What!"

" — and what were you doing going through my things?"

"Jesus Christ, back up a second! I wasn't going through any-thing — does that even *sound* like me to you? It was in the trunk of your car next to the groceries." And as soon as it popped up, the anger in her subsides as she sits idly on the mattress across from me, watching the shadows on the wall.

"Why is everything about sex?" I venture, " — I don't even really care about sex! I've gone without it all year without any complaints, haven't I? It's *you* — *you* who's afraid of it, *you* who won't talk about it and who makes it out to be this big, scary thing. What are you even afraid of?"

Nothing. I sit there and I wait, but there's nothing — not even on her face or in her lost, distant eyes.

"Why *don't* you want to talk about it?"

Allie shakes her head abruptly. "No. I'm drunk," she says, mutter-ing. "I'm drunk!"

"Well, so am I."

"No," she says, shaking her head with finality. "No."

"No, what, goddammit?"

"It's impossible!" she shouts, grabbing her head with both her hands. "Impossible to say what I mean!" And then all at once her arms collapse by her side and her body goes limp, as if she's about to tip over. Allie remains quiet, motionless, and hangs over like a rag doll on the bed before finally looking up at me with thick, glossy eyes. "Sean … " she whispers, taking me by the hand, " — can we talk about this tomorrow? … Please?"

Allie looks on the verge of tears but I still have to grit my teeth and try like anything just to keep from exploding. Why must I be made to feel ridiculous over wanting answers to something that so obviously demands them?

"Please," she says, nearly whimpering, petting my fingers with her hands. "Please … "

"It's just … " And my voice drifts off before I can really start. I take a deep breath and try to center myself before continuing. "I'm just trying to understand — the best I can — why you feel the need to keep so much distance from me, Allie. It's just *me*." I look into Allie's eyes and rub her hand back with mine, but she looks away, despondently, and doesn't appear to be listening. "It's just ... all I want ... all I've *ever* wanted, is for you to let me in—for me to understand you."

"Oh right," she says sarcastically, rolling her eyes, "—so you're on a quest for knowledge now, is that it?"

"Allie, will you just listen to me?" Allie doesn't pull away, but I can feel her hand recoil in mine—can see the burning coals roasting behind her eyes. "I just want to understand. The rest doesn't matter," I say. "The rest you can talk to me about ... tomorrow."

Allie says nothing for a long time, and all I can hear are random sparks crackling up from the embers in the dying fire. Pretty soon, I'm gonna have to turn off the air conditioning.

"I bought them ... " But then she quietly exhales before looking up at me again. "—I bought them for me. For me alone."

" ... *Why?*"

"Because I needed them."

"For what?" I ask, but then Allie just sighs, exasperated. She looks at the wall.

"—Do you trust me, Sean?"

"What?"

"I said," and she looks up at me, "do you trust me?"

"Of course I do, Allie."

Allie stares into my eyes, as if searching for something I don't have the courage to say. She looks at me for a long time before finally relaxing, looking down at our hands again, and even playing gently with my fingers. "I do let you in, Sean," she says, softly. "More than you know. But please ... trust me? Tomorrow I'll try to explain it the best I can ... But tomorrow—and not now—okay?"

And there's nothing left for me to say, except "okay" back to her, and I kiss her hand in acceptance. "I understand," I say. "Tomorrow."

10

That night Allie sleeps in my arms and I have dark dreams of a man I don't recognize. His skin is smooth and faintly luminescent, glowing soft and gold in the darkness, and he is dancing, dancing. His face, framed by long black hair, is beautiful, effulgent, but terrible all at once — like the attraction of a moth before its consumption in a flame. His ankle bells jingle and play with his effortless, dramatic steps while bangles and bracelets wreath their way up his arms like flowering vines, and all the while he is looking at me — watching me as he dances softly in the darkness — beckoning me into his great and ultimate destruction. I want nothing more than to join with him, to dance in his dance, but it's all too much, all just beyond me — sometimes I think everything's beyond me. The man steps and he gestures to me incomprehensibly, always gestures I can't understand, and I want to look away — but I can't. So I sit, and I watch — watch him dance softly alone in the darkness; like distant summer lightning crying silently in the night.

And then I wake up. My arms empty and my bed a mess, I hear the shower running, but my dim, vacant brain is too awash in sleep and dream to come to the obvious conclusion until Allie comes in later, drying her shining wet hair in the cool morning light.

"Rise and shine, silly," she says, and leans in to give me a good-morning kiss before shooing me off to take a shower myself.

The hot water steams off my body like mist billowing on a bog, and my hands wash my frothing hair mechanically. What happened last night? I ask myself. And why did it matter? But the only sense I can find is in the hissing of the high-pressured water and the steam that it emits.

Wasn't there something? I ask myself. Wasn't it important? But my brain only buzzes dully. The words "Devil's Path" rise steadily to me out of the steam like a revelation. The word "cats"; the word "kills."

And suddenly I think of Allie, of Allie in the heat of it all. I think of fire and wine — the stench of stale liquor. *In Vino Veritas*. Jack and Coke, she said. "Your favorite, isn't it?"

My favorite. Is it? But I can't remember. Can't remember why anything as senseless as a drink mix would ever matter to me. So I stare into the steam and think harder, think and watch as things rise out of the steam at me like offerings: rich people waltzing and chard when I wanted chicken.

But why would I ever want a thing like chicken?

And out of the steam Allie comes to me as if from behind a veil, her body wet and naked in the falling water. She takes me in and locks me in her embrace, her eyes never reaching mine. Her hands wrap around my neck, her exposed legs about my hips. I look for her in her eyes but can't find them, and can only watch as her head droops back, back behind her like an overripe flower. I look harder for her, look for her in her eyes, but only watch as they roll back in her head. Her eyelashes bead up with steam like dew and flutter like wings as she moans to me, deeply in the middle of the hissing of the hot steam.

"Ohhh," she moans. "Ohhh."

And in the midst of her moaning the hissing grows spontaneously and overtakes us, filling my ears like the ocean. I try to shout in the sound but my call is only lost in its thrall.

"Ah!" I keep shouting. "Ah!" But all I can see is Allie's "ohhh," her eyes long lost to me entirely.

"Ohhh," her mouth silently calls to me, with the hissing in my ears. "Ohhh…"

And that's when I'm awake for real, lurching spasmodically from the drowning sleep, shouting aloud in its passing.

"Huh?" Allie asks, looking about. She looks almost as scared as me, but only for a moment. "Sean?" she calls, but all I can do is lie back in the sheets and pant out my relief in bursts.

"God," I breathe heavily. "My God."

"Was it a nightmare?" I hear her asking me, but it's all far, far away from me.

"No," I say, feeling an intense, warm buzzing at the crown of my head. "I don't think so." And slowly I feel the tingling running up my spine, cool and wonderful like a current. My crown buzzes excitedly, charged by the power in my spine. I smile and feel myself sink into the mattress, feel myself melt into it like a mirage.

"Mmm," I hear Allie humming quietly, "a dream then."

"Allie?" I ask, smiling to her from beneath the sheets.

"Hmm?"

"Why don't you come move in here with me?"

1 1

Wʜᴇɴ ɪᴛ ᴄᴏᴍᴇs ʀɪɢʜᴛ down to it, I don't think I was made for these times—this age of serial monogamy. Start one relationship, let that go on for some time, and when that ends, well, it was fun while it lasted—find someone else to help fill up the gaps. I think at my core I've always been too old-fashioned, too sensitive, too goddamn girly, but girls have always been the ones who've caused me the most trouble to begin with, so I don't even know what the hell I am. Lonely, idealistic, empty—find the adjective that fits, I don't care.

Even *before* we started dating, I didn't believe that Allie could ever like me. She was too beautiful for me, I thought, too smart. When she did like me, I cherished it as something that would inevitably pass. Allie could never love me, I believed, would never stay with me. Why would she? It was something I could only enjoy while it lasted. And then it did last, and before I knew it, she did love me. But how? Why? And why me? Why not somebody else—somebody more attractive, better, stronger, smarter? Someone not as stupidly ordinary as me.

The first time Allie ever told me she loved me was the day I thought she was going to dump me—with her foot pressing the brake and her hands at ten-and-two. I thought things were over, but a miracle happened that day, and things continued. Things went on.

But then what? What next? So she loved me—but for how long? A week? A month? A year? Ten? And then what?

Allie may have told me that she loved me, but I didn't believe it, never *really* believed it. Allie was always so distant, so obscure. She never wanted to talk about herself, never wanted to talk about anything *real*. I barely even saw her the first six months we dated. There was always something, some perfectly legitimate, reasonable excuse at the ready — oh, the literary magazine's meeting tonight; yeah, sorry, I'm so tired tonight, I think I'm just gonna call it a night; actually, we planned it to be a kinda girls' night out sorta thing; thanks for being so understanding, Sean. I'll talk to you later; *I love you*. Always tacked on at the end there, just in case I forgot. Just in case I thought about raising mutiny.

Sometimes I used to think that sex would make me feel better about everything. Sex would lend me a kind of emotional security, I reasoned, but then Lily would pop shortly into my mind and remind me just how tenuous that seeming security could be. Allie never did explain to me why she was so opposed to sex. "If I were not myself," she told me that first time. "If I were free." As if that actually meant something. As if it were anything more than some recitation, some pretentious quotation from some great, profound literary work to keep her from actually having to confront an issue head-on, for once.

I guess it was thoughts like these that eventually got me thinking: maybe if we lived together things would be different; maybe things would change. Sharing our lives together would ground her, I imagined — would make her descend from her ivory-tower fantasies and root her in the mundane banalities of an intimate, sustained relationship. Sitting on my bed in my old dorm room with Ivan playing solitaire across the way, I used to stare at the wall, visualizing Allie there before me: Allie, drifting placeless through the town, coming to my room in the middle of the night wearing sunglasses and a sundress; Allie, sitting on logs, in the woods, reciting poetry, with her eyelids fluttering; Allie, dancing in a palace; dancing. Would living with Allie change her? Would it change me? Maybe I'd finally feel … I don't know … *okay* about everything. It didn't take long for the thoughts to start creeping into my mind — three months into our relationship, maybe four. Our first summer passed — a season that started with Allie, inexplicably drunk, bumping into me in the woods, and ended with a miracle when she told me she loved me. Autumn came, and with it, the cold; it was the coldest autumn in all my memory.

The day the thought first came to me we had been walking down Hasbrouck, down toward the park, just across from the old clock tower. That's when the bells tolled, just as we walked by, their ringing cutting crisp through the cold October air, like glass. A cold snap was what they were calling it, but those of us who had already made it through our first winter in the valley knew better: dark tidings; worse things to come.

That afternoon we were walking out across the Hasbrouck field, down toward the gazebo at the far corner when the deep tong of the bell finally sufficed at four. Me, I was looking out at the mountains: across the valley, low clouds sank heavily upon the ridge like sea phantoms.

"Mmm," Allie hummed lightly, her arm interlocked with mine, "look at that." You can always tell the weather in the valley by the clouds on the ridge: they always stop there for some time, readying themselves patiently before they hone in for the kill.

"So your mom's moving away tomorrow then," I said, carefully intonating nonchalance, "isn't she?" But it was more a statement than it was a question, and my words hung about in the air like the clouding of my breath.

"Yeah," Allie said, bundling up closer to me, "tomorrow is right." She sighed and rubbed her hands briefly with mine—for the warmth, I suppose.

"Finished, it's finished," she said, looking at me with a sly smile, "—nearly finished, it must be nearly finished." And with that we entered the gazebo and sat down on its middle bench. Somehow, even if we were still outdoors, the illusion of enclosure made us feel warmer.

"So," I asked, "what about all your stuff?"

"My stuff?" Allie was looking up at the trees, observing the stark yellows and reds of the leaves and how interestingly they contrasted against the dull weight of the gray-white sky.

"Well, your house has got to be full of it, doesn't it?"

"Her house," she corrected, suddenly paying attention, "—and no. I stripped that place bare the moment I first left."

After that we sat in silence for some time. Down from the ridge, the clouds were descending upon the valley, its foggy gray advance murking forward like a demon in a dream; the wind was getting worse.

"Let's go inside somewhere," I said, shivering. "I'm freezing."

"Just stay with me a little longer," she said, rubbing my arm with her hand. "Then we can go back to your dorm."

"On the other side of campus? Your dorm is right here—let's just go to yours." But the cold howl of the wind picking up high from the woods behind us was all I got as an answer. I looked over at Allie, but she was staring off at the nothing of the sky. No matter how much Allie pretended to not care, it was obvious how much her mother was on her mind. I always wondered why Allie seemed to hate her mom so much. Hate is the wrong word though, I suppose. Utter distaste? Something more along those lines.

Allie suddenly frowned and looked at me intently, as if reading my thoughts. "I can't stand her, and I never could," she said. Allie always referenced her mother with the most impersonal pronoun she could muster. Mother was only "mother" when the confines of grammar demanded it, but otherwise she was always a "she," her title rarely elevated above that of a "her." Sometimes even an "it"—and if Allie could spare the pronoun altogether, she would.

"Even when my dad was alive, I still couldn't stand it." Her father was always different. Always referenced in hushed, reverential tones.

Even at the time, I knew Allie was trying to tell me something. It wasn't every day that Allie mentioned things that actually pertained to the concrete history of her life—Allie was trying to tell me something deep, something profound; she was trying to make some kind of connection with me; she was opening up to me, for once; she was letting me into her private world of secrets and mysteries. But sitting there in the moment, the only question I could manage was the most obvious one—the one question I had asked countless times by then—each time, perhaps, hopelessly hoping for an explanatory answer: "Why don't you like your mother?"

But Allie just shrugged, as if there were nothing to it—as if everyone hated their mothers for the purported reasons she gave. "Sometimes the people you like the least are the people you have no special reason to," she said. "You just do."

It was something I had heard variations of before, although that time around I really sat and grappled with it, struggling to place myself inside the head of a person who would hate—not just dislike—their mother for simply rubbing them the wrong way. "What?" I wanted to say, "something about her just pisses you off?" As usual, I kept my stupid mouth shut.

"I know you think I'm hiding some dramatic sob story, but I'm really not," she continued, looking up at me. "She's just ordinary. Too ordinary. She's the most ordinary person I've ever met, and it makes me sick. I never knew what daddy saw in it; daddy could've done much better."

Daddy. I practically ignored every other word she said. *Daddy*! The very *sound* of it stupefied me. Questions raced through my head, first about her father, and then — once I had enough time to think — about her mother. Too *ordinary*? Did Allie really have the audacity to claim — even though the poor woman had given birth to her — that daddy could have done better? But then there was that word again ... *Daddy*.

"I loved him."

She *loved* him! The very notion was almost as shocking as the word "daddy." As if the love between a daughter and a father were anything to be shocked about. But it was *Allie*, and she *loved* him, and it was a love I could *believe* in. How did he do it? What was the secret? What kind of man was he? What size shoe did he wear?

"Daddy was the best. He's the one who showed me the whole area, who first brought me to the mountains and the caves. We used to go camping almost every weekend, if the weather was right. He was the one who first taught me how to start fires." I never knew until then that Allie knew how to start fires. We had never gone camping before, even when the weather had been right.

"You know we're sitting on his bench?" I suddenly found myself having to shake myself out of a self-involved trance, realizing that Allie was in fact asking me a question, and a weird one at that.

" —I'm sorry, his what?"

"His bench," she said. "They dedicated it to him after he died."

"Why would they dedicate a bench to him?"

"Because he was a professor here at the school."

"Oh ... "

Allie showed me the plaque, a plain bronze thing that read "IN MEMORY OF TERRENCE DONOWITZ." No dates, no explanations.

Allie then went on to list his great litany of achievements: literature professor; chairman of the English department; published poet; once published a short story in *Harper's* magazine; teaching excellence awards — and that wasn't nearly the end of it. He fought and was wounded in the Vietnam War during his second tour of duty; was a big-game hunter who used to teach Allie how to track deer in the woods (even *this* Allie seemed prideful about, in spite of her vegetarianism); and all this before he turned fifty-two. Then he died, and all that was left was a bench dedication in the park across from the old clock tower.

"I'm half expecting you to tell me that he ran with the bulls, too," I said, and for once, Allie actually laughed at one of my half-baked attempts at a literary reference.

"I'm half surprised he didn't."

Great. So the only other person in this world that Allie also seemed to love was Ernest Hemingway. Go figure.

After that we didn't speak for a few moments. The wind was picking up even more than before from the woods behind us, and I was just sitting there, thinking about everything: about deer hunting and bull running and little ordinary me getting gored in a Spanish alleyway. But that's when Allie spoke again.

"He killed himself," she said, and was looking at the ground.

"…What?" I couldn't believe she was actually offering me this information. I hadn't even asked. I only wish I could've offered up something more than my lame replies in return.

"When?"

"I was…" Allie paused, catching her voice in her throat. She was still looking away at the ground. "—I was fifteen. And not at home when it happened."

And as much as I couldn't believe she was offering me this information, another part of me couldn't believe she had never told me before. Did this mean I had passed some sort of test? That she finally trusted me enough to tell me something worth talking about? Only, now that she *did* tell me, what more was left for me to say?

"I'm sorry…I didn't know."

"Yeah," she said lowly, "I know…" The wind whistled violently through the trees and caught Allie's long blonde hair aloft in its path. "I never found out why he did it," she said, her hair whipping in the breeze. "He never left a note…Never even gave me a warning."

"So you just…don't know?"

Allie sighed and looked off at the ridge again, but there was nothing to see but the heavy gray of the clouds rolling out into the valley.

"What did your mom…"

"—Have you ever read *Heart of Darkness*, Sean?" she asked, cutting me off.

I blinked a few times, asking myself whether she was really asking me a literary question, or if I was perhaps just imagining it instead. "…No, Allie, I have not read *Heart of Darkness*."

"In *Heart of Darkness* a man tells us—the readers—about a

time that he listened to another man tell a story about *another* man named Kurtz. Kurtz is downriver in the Congo, where he's lost his mind and his methods have become…unsound. The first man listens to the whole story, and the second man wonders what could have led Kurtz to the brink of insanity. We get all the way to the end of the story, and with Kurtz on his deathbed, finally we hear his last words: 'The horror—the horror!' The person telling the story about Kurtz finally realizes—he *understands*—that it was the *horror* of everything that represented the *truth* of that insanity—but do you know what?" Allie stopped, looked at me, and apparently expected me to humor her.

"What?" I said, relenting.

"The *truth* is that the man's 'realization' was just his *interpretation* of what happened—nothing else. Kurtz didn't *tell* him, 'it was the horror of this place that did it to me,' he just said, 'the horror—the horror!' Everything after that—that was just the man's take on what happened."

" …I don't understand what you're trying to tell me, Allie."

Allie sighed and leaned her face on one of her hands, as if bewildered by my inability to grasp the apparent obviousness of her literary explication. "I'm just saying, Sean …sometimes the things you wish you could know the most are unknowable."

I sat and thought about what Allie said to me, until I realized I had no idea what she was talking about. But how could I say a thing like that? I didn't have the courage; and it was in that very unlikely of moments that the thought drifted to me, finally, as if from outer space: Allie and I, living together. Get her tied in with me; get her settled down; bind her life to mine; make it *real*.

"Allie?"

"Hmm?" she hummed lightly, as if the entire conversation we had just had never even took place. "You want to go back to your dorm?"

"Why don't we hang out more often?"

" …What do you mean?"

"I feel like I never see you."

Allie spoke with affection. "You see me all the time, silly."

"Not really. We live on the same campus and I see you maybe twice a week."

Allie didn't really respond. She just kind of looked at the ground some more, rubbed her shoes idly together. I was about to say something else when she finally said that she was just "busy most of the time," of course. "That's all."

"It's just that…" My voice drifted off.

"Just that what?"

"…Just that I feel like I barely know you sometimes."

Allie looked at me coldly and removed her arm from mine. "Don't say that," she said lowly.

"It's just… how I feel… I'm sorry."

But Allie only sighed and bent forward and rubbed at her face. She stared off at nothing, for a long, long time.

"Sean," she said, finally looking up at me, "—*nobody* knows me better than you." Her gaze fixed itself upon me and didn't leave, leaving me to do nothing but accept the enormity of her stare and all the honesty it expressed; and her eyes were trembling in that dark gray afternoon light—trembling as she looked at me with a vulnerability I hadn't seen in her before. When she spoke again, it was nearly in a whisper.

"Don't you *know* that?"

I had nothing to say, and apparently, neither did she. Allie just sat there, bent forward with her arms crossed, staring off into nowhere as I sat next to her, asking myself if it were really possible that of all the people on the planet, it was somehow me who knew Allie Donowitz the best. What on earth did I even *know* about her? That she grew up here? That she liked hiking, was obsessed with poetry, hated her mom and that her dad killed himself—the latter two for indeterminate reasons?

"Listen…" she started. "I know you're cold and everything, but let me show you something." Allie looked to me and unbelievably, smiled. "I *want* to show you something."

I looked into Allie's smile, and it was difficult for me not to smile back. She wanted to show me something? It could only mean one thing: another place; another adventure; another *secret*—it was an offer I couldn't refuse.

"Okay."

"Okay," she repeated, smiling. "Okay." Allie got up from the gazebo bench; she motioned with her eyes, showing me that it was time for us to go into the woods. "Come on," she said, "this way." And with that, we went off together. Just like old times.

The air shifted when we entered the woods. The spaces closed, the fog rolled in and somehow, something changed. Allie had her hands in her jacket pockets, her shoulders hunched as she led me through the fog to our destination unknown. I tried to keep up, but even after the first few moments, I was already lagging behind, struggling to make it over underbrush and through bushes as Allie traipsed along and ahead, obviously having done this many times before. She brought me forward and only stopped when we reached a small clearing, the thickening air curling about our ankles. I stopped, too, and stooped over a little, trying to catch my breath. Allie just looked down at me, as if in sympathy.

"You know," she said, "I know you wish you could see me more often, and really, I do understand that—but intimacy isn't always about how physically close two people are … It just isn't."

"The world would be a lot simpler that way," I said, wiping the sweat from my forehead, watching my breath cloud in the air. "It should be a mathematical equation: two times two is four."

"I mean it though. You know that, right?"

I breathed deeply and finally nodded to her in acknowledgement. "Of course I do."

Allie looked at me, as if not quite believing me, and then turned and kept going. "Like I know this one girl, Rachel," Allie restarted, moving ahead with me following behind, "—and Rachel, Rachel was going out with this poor guy, Adam, from the city for over a year, and the whole time he's down there and she's up here, she's cheating on him—go figure. No qualms whatsoever. Then this last summer the poor guy moves up and transfers here, just to be close to her. Good guy, right? Feel sorry for him yet? Barely a week into the semester, and he cheats on her. So it goes—I only wish I could've been there to watch it happen, if only to revel in its poetry. I saw her just yesterday, too, right here in these very woods. I asked her how she was, she tells me 'okay.' 'I'm still looking for The One,' she tells me, 'The One.' Yeah, I said, aren't we all? Makes me sick."

I did little more than watch my feet. Allie wandered on through the fog with speed, hardly even looking to where she stepped, her arms waving about as she continued to speak.

"People make up their own mythic, fairy-tale fantasies—conjure up romantic, delusional narratives they are only too willing to live by: God helps the ones that help themselves, so live every moment to the fullest, never let an opportunity pass you by, spend the nights you'll never remember with the people you'll never forget, and—don't forget—*always* follow your bliss. It makes me goddamn *sick*, Sean, sick! All lies—stinking, crooked lies that people lap up, lap up and are only too keen to love and embrace until one fine day when they finally go careening headfirst into the limitations of reality, one fine morning when they wake up to the truth of it all.

"Just take what happened between you and Lily, for example." My ears perked up then, but I was only too quick to look at my feet again and avoid her gaze. I didn't know what she was talking about, frankly. Why did she have to bring Lily into it? I didn't like talking about Lily, much less thinking about her, and Allie knew that. What did Lily have to do with anything?

"I sat back and watched Lily pull that same routine on *four* guys before you, Sean, *four*! They'd all last about a month. They'd all do the same thing: meet her at her place, fall for her, hang around her every beck and call, and then the moment she got distracted she'd dump them on the spot and never even let them know that she had. You were number five, Sean—*five*! And that's only counting guys I directly knew about! Can you believe it? I would've done anything to have seen things happen the other way around, just for once. Just one time."

"Yeah," I said, "you actually told me that the first night we met."

"Yeah," she said, suddenly looking at her feet too. "Well, there you have it then."

I was silent for a long time after that. I didn't want to talk about Lily, I wanted to forget about her. At the same time, Allie had gotten so riled up about it—I felt like it justified an intelligent, articulated reply from me. Only there was a big, fundamental problem: I had *no* idea what the heck she was talking about.

" …I don't understand what you're trying to tell me, Allie."

Allie sighed and crossed her arms to close herself off from the wind. "I'm trying to tell you I'm not like that, Sean." But then as we walked deeper in the woods, winding our way through the fog between the trees, she said, "I don't know what I'm trying to tell you." I was surprised by that. It was the first time I had ever really questioned her, and it was the first time she ever really had no reply.

"Language is just a construction," she said, shrugging, talking almost to herself, "—grammatically designed to create the illusion of a linear, teleological trajectory; of an impending, musical resolution that doesn't actually exist in reality. Language only refers to itself; language actually is useless." Right, I thought. Then why bother telling me all that nonsense to start with? Why bother bringing me out to the wilderness to recite poetry if it's so useless? But after that, Allie was quiet; after that, Allie didn't speak anymore.

When we emerged from the woods on the other side, we came out onto a road I had never been on before. The houses were older here than they were in the rest of town, with big Victorians and Colonials packed in close to the sidewalks and elm trees lining the street. The street looked deserted, with the fog and the wind and the cold. The street looked haunted.

"Come on," Allie said, motioning with her head. "This way." But I didn't know which way "this way" was. North? South? I had lost my way back in the woods. I was in a tiny little town and I didn't even know where I was; all I could do was continue to follow Allie, to wherever she was going. How did she find her way through the woods in the fog? I looked ahead to where she was walking—five houses on, the street was swallowed up in dense, gray darkness, and then nothing more. But then Allie would never lose her way in this town, on this street, in those woods, even if there was fog. Allie was at home—and as much as I was a third-year, I was in her territory.

"Where are we?" I finally asked.

"Near the river," she said, as if that explained everything, "and now we're here."

The house we stopped at was a massive Victorian, its windows gazing out at us like eyes, its roof looming up from the fog like a tower. Out on the front porch, the swing bench creaked wildly in the wind to greet us in our arrival. I already knew where we were; there was only one place it could be.

"My home," Allie said lowly, " ... or at least it used to be ... once. Now she's in there all alone."

I stood there in silence, looking up at the house that had once been Allie's and now was *hers*. The wooden siding was a dirty off-white—looking like it had been smeared with grime and mold and left unchecked for years—and lined with scarlet red gables. The columns were stained with smatterings of yellow-green mildew; shingles were dangling loosely from the rooftops. I wondered how long things had been that way. I wondered if the next person would clean it up and make it all better again.

Could one woman really live in a house that big alone? I looked
it over closely, from the gleaming, wet weathervane to its darkened
cellar windows — it was grandiose enough to house a family of six
or seven, much less three. I stood there, silently, taking in the house,
and imagined what it must mean, to live in a place like that, on one's
own — imagined the cold draft that would sneak in under the heavy
wooden doors at night and the noises it would make.

"It must be lonely."

"I don't blame her for finally moving," Allie said, looking up at the
house above us. "I don't blame her, for that."

"I see," I said, nodding slowly, looking out at the house. "I think
I understand." And for once, I think I really did. Allie looked at me
and smiled: she believed me.

"Good," she said, and came in close, closer to kiss me softly and take
me in her arms and hug me. She was warm. Even in spite of the cold
and the damp and the memories of the past, Allie was warm.

When she parted from me, Allie silently started making her way
back toward the woods, but I hung back behind for a few moments,
my hands in my pockets, looking at my shoes. The wind picked up
again and I shivered and felt the hairs at the nape of my neck stand
on end, as if there were someone else there — as if there were someone else, watching me. I looked down the street, toward the woods,
but all I saw was Allie walking, with the gray fog beyond. I looked
in the other direction and saw nothing but the swallowing darkness,
the strength of the wind howling lost secrets to me as it tore through
the leaves in the trees — as it swept through tended lawns and dressed
them wet with fog. Finally, I looked up, where I knew I should have
from the start — up at the house — and saw *her*, looking down at me
from above; her face, white, cast just barely alight in the third-floor
window; her hand, upraised, touching the edge of the glass with the
lingering tips of her fingers.

A chill ran down my spine as our eyes met — me from below, she
from above — and saw her gaze stare not out at Allie down the way
but at me, only at me, emotionless, expressionless and empty. The
wind roared in protest and sent the leaves at me from the trees in a
whirlwind, spun them around and about me in a cyclone before carrying them off again, down the road, into the encompassing darkness.
I didn't know what to do, what to say — didn't even want to so much
as move. Allie's mother didn't look how I expected her to. Her hair

was long, unfurling in red curls down past her shoulders. Her skin was white; her skin was pale. And somehow, in the midst of it all, she was saying something to me. Somehow, she was there.

Snow came. I saw it in my eyes as I was looking up at her: silently at first, floating down from the indiscernible clouds above like suspended spirits, and thick and dense only a moment later. I looked around me as the snow fell on the deserted road, on the deserted house—watched as it coated the still-changing leaves and entombed them all in shimmering white. I looked back at the window one last time, if only to say goodbye, but she was gone already. In the end, I was too late.

"Look at this!" I heard Allie yell from the end of the road. "It's so beautiful!"

I made my way down the street, my feet already crunching into the sticking snow on the asphalt. "Would you look at this?" she said, her arms outstretched, her face fixed upward upon the sky's dim oblivion. "—In the middle of fall, no less!"

"Allie."

No response.

"Listen."

"Yesss?"

"Just before ... by the clock-tower ... you told me that sometimes the things you wish you could know the most are the things you'll never know ... something like that." But Allie appeared to not hear me, or at least not care. "What did you mean by that?"

"Sometimes things are just unknowable," she said, distracted, "that's all."

"Yeah, but your dad ... "

"Never mind that, never mind!" Allie was grinning at me. "Don't take me so seriously, Sean—look at this snow!" I looked at the snow; it looked as I expected it to. "Look at the way it looks with the leaves!" I looked, but couldn't even see the leaves or their colors anymore. It was all just white—monochrome—gone.

"You know what we should do? We should drive out to the Mohonk and watch the snow come down on the valley from the ridge!"

" ... What? You won't be able to see anything."

"What do you mean?"

"Look at the fog. Look at the clouds. With the snow? Forget it. You'd just see a mass of gray and white." Allie just frowned at me. "Besides, it's dangerous to go driving up the mountain in this weather."

"What about the clock tower?" she asked.

"What about it?"

"I have the keys to the rooftop; we could watch the snow fall from there."

"How the hell did you get those?" I asked, but she ignored my question altogether.

"It would be sooo pretty up there, and we could watch the snow fall on the changing leaves and it'd be beautiful."

"Allie, would you look around? Are you seeing the same street as me? I can't see ten freakin' feet with all the fog and snow. I didn't even know you could *get* fog and snow at the same time—we'd go up there and see absolutely *nothing*. And it's *freezing* out."

"Oh come *on*, Sean," she said, scowling before walking off again, back toward the woods. "It's gorgeous outside, the snow's covering the changing leaves, and all you want to do is go back to my dorm and make out."

" …What are you *talking* about?"

"Don't take this out on me!" she snapped. " —Why is everything *always* about *me*?"

Everything kind of moved in a blur after that. Allie was walking, and then she was up in the air; she had slipped. I went to grab her, but was too late, and then all I could hear was the *snap* breaking through the air like a thunderclap. Then there was the shouting and the screaming; Allie writhing on the ground like a wounded animal with her foot twisted in the wrong direction. She was screaming so loud; my hairs went on end she was screaming so loud.

"Call an ambulance!" she kept yelling. "Call an ambulance, Sean!"

I had my phone out, but got no reception. The only time I'd ever not gotten reception in town, and I was getting no reception. Allie, of course, didn't own a phone.

"I've got no reception," I said in a panic.

"What do you mean you've got no reception!"

"I've got no reception!"

"Go get somebody then! Go get somebody!"

"I'll go knock on your mom's door," I said, and turned to go and run.

It's hard to say what happened next. In one moment, Allie had gone from walking to slipping to falling, with her foot hanging limply like a lifeless, spent vessel. Then I offered to go get her mother—and the next thing I knew Allie was screaming again, almost worse than before, wildly like the wind itself, grabbing at my leg, gripping madly at my jeans, screaming at me, "NO!" and "NO!" I froze, feeling the stopping of time itself, and it was difficult for me to move — to turn back to face Allie, hanging to my legs with her face flushed in the cold; to look at her from above, and see all I was leaving behind: Allie, sprawled on the smeared, wet pavement, clinging desperately to my ankles, panting pathetically with her short little breaths withering wearily in the sky.

"No," she kept saying, with her dangling, twisted ankle. "No, no, no, no, no, no, no."

12

THE MOUNTAINS WERE DARK that day, and the clouds were everywhere—but not always. I walked out on the rock-ledge lookout and
watched the clouds bellow and breathe—watched them grow and die.
The valley was a mass of darkness: the gray, heavy moisture blowing
around and about me, hanging wet on the edges of my eyelashes like
dewdrops. And then only a moment later, it was gone—the cloud
would pass as it had come, and suddenly I could see the treetops and
the mountains—could see into the depths of the valleys. And even
in the sun's naked, ever-watchful glare, still, little remnants of clouds
hung about the trees and curled about the pines like lost dreams upon
waking. The valleys looked so deep from up there. The trees glistened
soft and wide with wetness and light. I wondered if I'd ever be able
to make it across to the other side—wondered if I'd be able to look
back from the mountain across the way, point with my finger and say,
"I was there. Now I am here. I made it through, across the valley." I
only hoped the weather would allow it.

That's when Allie appeared, out from the pine trees at the edge of
the rocks. She looked out at the valley briefly, but then the clouds
returned, emerging out of the depths in a deep sighing, forming an
impenetrable wall of gray—she never got a chance to see the valley
revealed. I looked at her and watched the way she watched the clouds,
like she understood them, somehow. Like she knew where they came
from—maybe even where they were going.

I don't know if I'll ever understand Allie. Looks like that, so small
and full of mystery and meaning. You can never tell with her. Looks

like that, it's like she hates the world. Or loves it. Or understands it and wishes she didn't — or doesn't understand it, although she thinks she does. I don't know — I can never tell. Mostly, I make up my own explanations, because I can never understand much of anything, although I wish I did. I don't think I'm stupid. I just think I'm simple.

"Have you ever studied art history?" She was looking at me now, smiling that smile she has, coming closer to me. I don't know why she asks me questions like that, when she already knows the answers to them.

"No."

"Just, looking out here at the clouds, being out here in the mountains, it reminded me of a painting. Two paintings, actually, both about Napoleon."

"Why Napoleon?"

"He was like a god," she said, looking out, admiring the wind, "but ultimately he was just a man. The two paintings are like that. One painting shows him like a giant, almost as big as his own horse, on the mountain, directing the wind with his hand, like a god. The other painting is this one by J.M.W. Turner, and it doesn't even show Napoleon, although it's about him. Just a horrible mountain and an even more horrible valley with a black cloud hanging over everything, bringing death and terror for these little tiny specks of people in the bottom corner."

I thought about that for some time, conjuring images of paintings I had never seen. Imagined the little specks getting consumed by the black cloud while I felt the wind at my back, while I felt the clouds and the wind move through me. Nature always scares me. I may love nature, but nature always scares me.

"What does it mean?" I finally asked.

"Well, it just makes you wonder, you know?" Allie continued to smile. "Can man make the wind move? Or is he at the wind's mercy? Is man a god, or is he just a man?"

"I don't know," I said. "What about woman?"

*   *   *   *   *

It's a long way to the Catskills; it's a long drive out of town. Campus is surrounded by dense woods on all sides, until you hit the river. Once you cross the bridge, you're in the low-lying wetlands. Once you cross those, you can make it to the Shawangunk Ridge. Only then, after you cross over the peak of the Mohonk Mountain, only then can you see the Catskills, looming sleepily off in the distance — a distance that still remains to be crossed.

Living in the valley can be spooky that way. I grew up on Long Island, a perpetually expanding mass of strip malls and parking lots that ends only with the abruptness of the ocean, but the valley's different. The valley is gradual; you don't realize change until it's already left you behind.

In the valley there is town, and in the town there is Main Street. The road swarms with college dropouts and tourists from the city — leaf-peepers, as they're locally known. The road is lined with college bars and yoga studios; you'd never know the valley was there at all.

But only a block apart from the one main road is Huguenot Street, a purportedly haunted strip of seventeenth-century houses, farms and graveyards. Walk off Main Street in one direction and you'll find Huguenot Street; walk off Main Street in the other direction and you'll find my house and the rail trail on Water Street. Beyond that there's nothing, there's no one. Only woods. God knows where campus is in that mess — an island of concrete in a sea of trees. Campus and Main Street are all we have; they are our bastions.

The world seems thin when you're in the valley, somehow — transient and fragile — as if you could stick your hand through it and reach over to the other side. If I walk down my road one way, I find my town. If I walk down my road the other way, I find something else — I find the woods. And behind my house, off the road entirely, is the river, flowing on silently, endlessly. I live in the borderlands; my house is the last outpost, a way station anchored to the river; always, always the river.

Sometimes, when it's nice outside, I sit on the shore and watch the water go by. Even when it's frozen, the water flows on unseen, beneath the surface. People tell me that it flows on and eventually merges with the Hudson; after that, it continues to flow on until it merges with the ocean. After that, who knows? Some people think the ocean has a finality to it, but I grew up by the ocean, so I know better. Oceans move; oceans speak.

That is where I lived. That is where I'm from.

But all that is in the past: the only thing in the valley that holds any weight, that bears any meaning. Historical signs inform me of Sojourner Truth, and how she spent her slave days on the banks of the same river I spend mine. Old stone houses are turned into museums and candles are lit for old graves while old, abandoned mining caves are left to rot and die. And through it all, the rail trail snakes and weaves along with the river and tells the tale of a time long gone. The valley is a place with no future, and a place with no future has no present; the valley is a place without presence.

But I am here. I am present. And I want a future. On the river. In my boathouse. On the border. Between this world and the next.

With my Allie.

…*Allie.*

Once we were in the woods together, walking, when I spoke. I told her the woods were frightening. The woods were very dark that night. Even with her holding my hand, I was more afraid than she knew.

"This is where I am," she told me that night. "This is where I'm from."

"I know," I said, "—but does it always have to be that way?"

Allie never gave me a worded reply.

But today we are leaving. Today we are going to the mountains, together. Only, it's a long way to the Catskills. It's a long way out of town.

*   *   *   *   *

The world is a very mysterious place.

*   *   *   *   *

Allie went back into the trees to make camp, and I don't know why, but I hung back for a long time, sitting on the rocks, watching the wind. When I finally rejoined her, Allie already had a fire going. Her skin was glowing warm and orange against the flames, and I marveled, thinking, has it only been a day? I brought my mind back to the night before—to Allie on the edge of the bed, the fire playing in her eyes, her green eyes, asking me if I loved her. If I really, really loved her. Had that ever really happened? Sometimes I'm not so sure.

"Don't mind me," she said, poking at the fire with her walking stick. "You should watch the sun. It's very pretty."

"I did," I said, walking over slowly. "The clouds were everywhere. You couldn't see a thing."

"Are you sure?" she said, looking deep into the fire. "You might want to look again."

All I had to do was look up from her to see that things had indeed changed; I didn't even need to go to the lookout. The sky was filled with light, the sun suspended low and red in the trees, its light dispersed and scattered in thin, humid beams, all merging in the warmth of the fire. Allie wasn't even looking—she only continued to play with the fire, somehow sensing the wonderment all around her from her own vantage point. I don't know how she does it, sometimes. Her back was turned the whole time.

I stood there for some time, admiring the light, listening to the crackling of the fire, observing the condensed moisture clinging to the tips of the pine needles, just as it had my eyelashes, little points of crimson light twinkling from them all. It wouldn't last long, I knew. Very soon, it would be dark, and the fire would be all we had left. The thought unnerved me. I don't like the dark.

"I'm going to make some coffee, if you want some." Allie poked at the fire with her walking stick. "Would you like some coffee?"

"Sure," I said, sitting next to her, "I'd love some."

"Mind getting the stuff out of my backpack? There should be a jar of coffee grounds and an empty plastic bottle."

I went over to her backpack and rummaged through, getting what she asked for. "What about the pot?" I asked. "I can't find the pot in here."

"No need," she said. "Those two things are fine."

"Okay." I handed her the grounds and the plastic bottle. Allie opened up the coffee grounds and threw two small handfuls of it into the plastic bottle, then unscrewed the top off her canteen and filled the bottle completely to the top with water, even letting it overflow a little before she closed it. I watched her carefully, still not quite understanding what she was doing. Allie tightened the top of the plastic bottle again, shook it up a bit, then put the whole thing right on top of the fire.

"Won't it melt?"

"There's no air inside," she explained to me. "If there's no air inside, it'll keep the plastic from melting." I stared into the fire, watching as the coffee brewed silently, the plastic indeed never melting. After a few minutes, Allie got me to fetch some mugs out of her backpack. Then she extracted the bottle from the fire with a towel, unscrewed the top, poured a bit of the coffee out in the dirt and then added some cold water to settle the grounds.

"All ready," she said, smiling, and poured each of us a mug. I held mine warm in my hands and blew the steam off before drinking; it was indeed coffee, brewed right out of an old Poland Spring bottle. I was totally amazed, and I didn't make it a point to hide it. It was magic.

"Sometimes the laws of nature aren't as concrete as they seem," she said, sipping from her mug. "Sometimes they bend."

*   *   *   *   *

"What?" she had asked me earlier this morning. "What'd you just ask me?" And I had to repeat myself, although it was very difficult for me—I had the intolerable, almost irrepressible urge to giggle.

"Really?" she had asked me. "Really, you mean that?"

"Sure," I had said.

"But why ... ? Why now, I mean?" But that was only after a long silence. I was still smiling to myself, smiling beneath the sheets. It seemed like a very silly question to me at the time, although now it seems perfectly reasonable. It kind of came out of nowhere. We had just come out of a weird, awkward kind of fight—condoms found clandestinely—and then all of a sudden I was asking her to move in with me.

But you know, the strangest thing about it is I just can't bring myself to take it back, to *want* to take it back—to take it back the way I'd take back the time I told Lily I loved her. I can't even say how many times I've wished away those words, how many nights I've stayed up, suffering in shame and self-loathing over those horrible, humiliating words.

Only, this time, something's different. This time, something's changed. And I can't bring myself to take it back. I can't even bring myself to want to—even in spite of Allie's silence. We've been on the road on the way to the Catskills for a whole half hour now, but there's been scarcely a word between us. We've driven up over the ridge already, descending down into the valley on the other side, the woods unknown, the trees unfamiliar—it's remarkable how much can change on the other side of a mountain.

I look over at Allie to see if she feels the same way, but she only stares ahead at the darkening trees, her hands at ten-and-two. Look deep enough into the green and you'll watch it turn red instead.

"I think I do want to move in with you," she had finally said, still lying apart from me on the bed. "I think I do."

"That's good," I said, almost laughing to myself. "That's great." She finally reached out and touched me then, taking my hand with both of hers, but my face was still buried deep in the sheets, and she couldn't see me. She was so serious about the whole thing. I kind of felt sorry for her. "It's just a game," I wanted to tell her. "Pay it no mind."

Only, the hours tread lightly, and mind moves in a flow. Sitting there in the car, all I feel is dizzy, like I got out of bed too fast—like I got out of bed too fast and now I've got a head rush. It's hard for me, suddenly. My hands end with their fingers and my feet end with their toes. I don't want to accept that, somehow. I want to dance naked in the moonlight and melt myself into the earth. An hour or two ago I might have done just that, only the moment's passing now, passing into mere memory, and the more time passes, the crazier that memory feels. Crazy but *right*—more *right* than anything else has ever felt in my entire life. It's hard for me to say a thing like that, but it feels right. It rings true.

Am I going crazy? The more time passes, the more it begins to feel that way. Only, I've never felt saner in my entire life than I did this morning, in that *moment*, that moment that's moving into memory, that moment when I asked Allie if she wanted to move in with me. "The sane man's insane," I would have said, "I am merely misunderstood." Only, now that's beginning to sound like the talk of a crazy person. Crazy people always think they're getting better.

"I'm not sure I should move in," Allie told me later, when she came back from the shower. "I'm just so…I just don't know if it'd be good for me."

"Well, do you want to?"

"There's a lot more to life than wanting to," she said, softly. "Life is never that simple."

"That's your choice." Allie looked kind of surprised by that one; I was moderately surprised myself, and I was the one who had said it. By not-speaking, I speak. By not-acting, I act.

"Life is all *about* choices, Sean."

"I know—that's my point."

By not-choosing, I choose. The thought makes me smile, even now. Only, Allie got a little angrier then. I don't think she was used to me talking to her that way.

"What, so now I should just forget everything? Forget the past, forget it all and just jump into a new life with you?"

"Don't you want to?"

She was silent for some time after that, sitting there on the edge of the bed with her back to me. She still didn't have her clothes on yet—she was still wrapped in her green towel from the shower, and the light was shining in on her shoulders from the window. She looked so beautiful. I wanted to tell her so, but I didn't. By choosing, I didn't choose. The moment was already passing.

" … Yes," she said, finally, her back glaring in the sunlight, "I want to."

But you can't, I thought. But you won't.

I could see into her thinking then, so clearly, in a flash. So many hours wasted, trying to think about her, trying to understand her, only to feel her in that moment when she flashed before my eyes—her mind, her works, her dreams, playing and dancing in my hands like a vision. By not-thinking, I saw. By not-trying, I did.

We leave everything. We go to my car and we leave forever.

We go north. We go north to Alaska, where no one knows my name. Sean sleeps much of the way, and when we arrive he wakes up and smiles. "We made it," he says. "We're here."

We build a home together. It is very cold, and the winters are very dark. In the spring I sleep much of the day, and Sean plants flowers in the garden and he eats his meals by the fireside.

In the last cool nights before the summer we walk together through open fields, and he holds my hand. I am no longer afraid. I no longer have to pretend.

In the summer, the wildflowers grow very bright; orange and yellow in effervescent bursts; pink and purple in iridescent beams. Sean sleeps in the dark, where the constant sunlight does not bother him, and I sit by the window, watching the white sky glow.

Out here, I feel free.

Only, thinking of the future like that never accomplished anything. Thinking of the future only eventually makes you think of the past—and those who only think of their past become slaves to it. I know, from experience, as does Allie. It's a very pretty picture, but even she knows it for what it really is: a lie.

The road bends off to the left, the mountains bare and exposed to us in the sloping distance, set off against the horizon at the end of it all. Only the locals know better; only the locals know there is something else on the other side.

The car slows down and eventually Allie pulls us over at a small, shanty road stop: "Top O' the Trail Deli," the weathered sign reads, but in a few years it will be too weathered to read anything at all.

"I need to get an aspirin," she says, finally turning to look at me. "Can I get you anything?"

"I would like some water," I say. "Some sweet water."

Allie looks at me questioningly, her left eyebrow raised above her sunglasses. "Sweet water?" She pauses, as if not knowing what to say. "If water's what you want, I filled the canteens before we left."

"Oh. Okay."

"You filled them, actually, now that I think about it."

"Yes, that's right."

Allie opens the door to leave but turns back one last time. "Are you sure you're feeling okay?"

"Yeah, I feel good," I say, nodding. "I feel well."

"Well," she says, weighing the word in her mind. She seems to like it, and after some time she looks up at me and kind of half smiles. "That's good." And then she shuts the door and walks away. I sit back in the seat and listen to the birds. A high-pitched bell jingles playfully as Allie walks through the deli's door, and then I hear the birds again. In the car it is very warm. I think I feel thirsty. Outside, there are little white flowers in the bushes by my window, and I can smell them and I can smell their pollen and I can hear and see the bees buzz on in the sunlight.

I never want this moment to end.

*   *   *   *   *

Allie was quiet much of the night, preferring to spend most of her time sitting by the open fire pit. It was very quiet that night, much quieter than I would've expected, camping way out in the wilderness like we were. I couldn't hear much more than the wood hissing and crackling in the fire. But all the while Allie just sat there, resting on a log, poking at the fire with her walking stick, watching the sparks rise. There wasn't a whole lot I could do, so I sat by the fire across from her, watching her out of the corner of my eye. It wasn't until it got very dark that she started speaking again.

"Hmm," she hummed, smiling lightly in the darkness, "I had such a strange dream last night."

"A dream?"

"Yes."

" … What was it about?"

"I had a dream that you were sitting in your restaurant, up in the front by the window in that big divan there, you know?"

Silence. Silence and crackling, and not a cricket to be heard.

"You were eating olives."

"Olives?"

"Yes. You were eating olives, and sitting across from you was this black cat, very small but sitting up with its front paws on the table. It would meow sometimes and brush its face with its paw, and then you'd toss an olive into its mouth. It was very cute. You looked very happy."

"I wonder what it meant."

"I don't know," she said. "Does it really have to mean anything? I don't put much stock in dream reading. My mom once got me a dream dictionary, but it was all nonsense. Teeth symbolize vanity and guns symbolize penises and all the rest of that stuff. The people who write those books don't understand the way symbols work. They try to reduce everything to signification."

"What are symbols, if not signs?"

"Mysterious." Allie let the word hang in the air. Let it rise with the sparks in the darkness.

"All I can remember," she said, looking into the fire, "at least, after that … was that you had lost something." Allie went quiet for a moment and poked at the wood with her walking stick. "You had lost something but came to the restaurant, looking for what you had lost, and found the cat and the olives there instead. By looking for what you lost, you found something else you didn't have before … you ended up happier than you were to begin with."

"So I lived happily ever after then?"

"For a little while," she said with a smirk. "I can't say for sure. I missed the ending when I woke up."

"You woke up." I measured the words patiently in my mind. Tried them on and saw how they felt.

"You woke me up, actually," she reminded me. "You were shouting pretty loud … I've never seen you shout like that before."

I almost replied but thought the better of it. What could I say? I thought back and remembered the dream. Remembered Allie approaching me naked from the steam and the charge I felt up my spine. But no matter how much I seemed to remember, the last thing I could do was bring myself back. It felt past. It felt crazy.

"What were you dreaming about?" she finally asked.

"I can't remember." A log split in the flames, broke into pieces and cried out defiantly into the night.

"You can't remember," she said, although it was not a question. Allie looked at me sideways through the fire, her head just slightly cocked to one side. She didn't believe me. Not for one moment.

"How about that?" she said. " … How about that."

"I need to go to the bathroom," I said, getting up from my rock. "I'll be right back."

"Yeah," she said, her gaze never leaving the fire. I heard her sigh deeply as I left. "Well … I'll be right here waiting for you when you do."

*　*　*　*　*

When Allie finally pulls in for a final stop at the trailhead and shuts off the car, I can't help but think of the railway trestle in High Falls; of Shaft 2A and the stockade and the helipad with the wildflowers all in bloom; of all that came before this time, this place, this moment. I remember Overlook Mountain with its burnt-down ruins; remember the old mining caves left gaping beneath the town above. It was so dark down there. You shut off your flashlight in a cave and the dark down there is unreal, is unearthly, and according to what Allie told me, the only place where real, absolute darkness exists. Yet you'd never even know the caves were there—you have to walk off the road, around a grated fence and down a path before you even find the entrances. You need a guide. You need a local to show you the way.

"I've never done this trail before," Allie says as we stand at the trailhead. "I've only heard what others have told me. It's supposed to be extremely hard. Very steep. Lots of good views."

I look around at the road, at the car one last time. The trailhead is so inconspicuous, it's amazing. It's just an ordinary paved road that dead-ends at some quaint-looking house. The opening to the trail is nothing but a two-foot gap in the house's wooden fencing. You'd never know. You'd just never even know.

"Well, it was a long enough ride," Allie says, smiling. "It's about time we finally got this trek started, wouldn't you say?"

I look ahead at the opening in the fence and can't help but smile myself. God knows what lies in store for me this time.

"Yeah," I say. "My thoughts exactly."

13

Wʜᴇɴ I ᴄᴏᴍᴇ ʙᴀᴄᴋ to the fireside, Allie is leaning forward on the log, massaging her temples with her left hand, the walking stick on the ground by her side. "You were gone a long time," she says.

"I know. You're never gonna believe what just happened to me."

"I'm sorry, Sean, but would you mind fetching me an aspirin out of my bag? This one's wearing off."

"Okay," I say, and go through her backpack to find it, although it's getting much harder to see. The fire's beginning to die down, and by the looks of it, it doesn't seem like Allie will be building it back up again anytime soon. Eventually I manage to find the aspirin, and when I do I hand them over to her and she dry swallows them.

Allie coughs and mutters lowly in the flickering light: "Once upon a midnight dreary, while I pondered, weak and weary ... " And then she looks up at me, smirks in spite of herself, and rubs her face with her hands. "God, I'm tired ... so very tired."

"Wanna call it a night?" I ask, but she only shakes her head.

"I'm fine," she says with annoyance, and then I see her bring a steel flask up from the shadows of her lap to the opening of her lips.

"That's not more coffee now, is it?"

"It's whiskey," she says.

"Whiskey."

"Whiskey," she repeats. " —Jack Daniels, left over from last night." She takes a sip and coughs and nearly gags. I stay where I am, across from her on the other side of the fire. I look closely at the flask and recognize it as my own—a birthday present from Steve, although I've hardly ever used it. And now Allie is.

"Oh, God." Allie rubs at her forehead. "I'm not used to alcohol. I can't even remember the last time I drank."

"Besides last night," I point out.

"Besides last night," she says, and despite everything, I see her smile faintly.

"Maybe we should go to sleep," I offer. "You really don't seem to be feeling too well."

"No," she says. "No." And then we don't speak again for some time. We sit back on our respective logs and watch the fire burn down to coals. Down to nothing. Allie, meanwhile, takes her drinks slowly, with long gaps in between.

"I came across a bear in the woods," I finally say. "That's what took me so long." Allie had her head down for some time, but now she lifts it steadily to meet my gaze.

"A bear?"

"Yeah. When I was going to the bathroom."

"What, just out here?"

"Yeah, just out there by the rock-ledge lookout."

"Why'd you go all the way out there?" she asks.

"I don't know. I hoped maybe I could see the valley … you know, in the moonlight."

"Did you?"

"No," I say. "Not at first. It was very dark. I couldn't see anything."

"So … what happened?"

"I don't know … I don't really know how to explain it. I had finished up and was out on the lookout with my flashlight, trying to see down into the valley, but the light would just fade in the fog, you know? In the clouds, and I couldn't see a thing. Just floating, kind of gaseous light glowing around my flashlight. Then I heard this rustling in the trees. I thought it must've been you, at first, but then I heard all these branches snapping. You could hear the tree trunks creaking. I shined my flashlight at the tree line at first and just stood there, absolutely still, watching the tree line sway. Then I shut off my flashlight. I don't know if that was the smart thing to do, but that's what I did. I couldn't bear the thought of actually seeing that thing, actually seeing it emerge from the tree line to look at me in the fog. So I shut it off. It was so dark then, Allie. So dark. It reminded me of the caves, you know? The caves in High Falls? I remembered what you said about absolute darkness—about it only existing in caves. I remembered thinking it was a crock of shit. But then I heard it. I heard it crunching through the woods, just lumbering on toward me, almost kind of patiently. And I still couldn't move."

"You didn't try to scare it? Not even with your flashlight?"

"No—I know that's what you're supposed to do. Even I know that. Scream and holler and jump up and down, right? But I don't know, I just couldn't do it. I couldn't see, couldn't move, could only hear. It came out from the trees and I could hear it on the rock, its paws, its claws, coming closer, always coming closer. It got so close to me at one point. So close I could smell it. And I couldn't even make a noise. I wanted to scream—I mean, what else can you do in that kind of situation? But I couldn't even do that much. I couldn't even manage out a noiseless whimper. I was trapped."

"So what happened? … It just went away?"

"It sniffed me. It sniffed at my hand and grunted once or twice, real lowly, you know? I could feel its nose testing my hand, kind of warm and wet, then it'd grunt and all I could do was just stand there, numb and paralyzed. I didn't know what it would do."

"So what *did* it do?"

The fire beckons from the charred and crackled logs, begging us on for more, but we only continue to sit there silently and watch it die.

"It left me alone," I say, finally. "—sniffed me a few more times and then it walked away."

"Walked away?" she asks.

"Yeah."

"It just walked away?"

"That's right."

"And then you came back here?"

"Yeah. And then I came back here."

Allie sits up straight for the first time since my monologue began. She sits up and regards me coldly in the darkening light, her hands playing with the flask in her grasp. I already know what's coming. I saw it coming way ahead of time.

"I don't believe you." Her voice is soft and low, and her eyes betray her true feelings already.

"You don't believe me."

"No. I don't believe you."

I rub my hands roughly in my lap, watching them instead of her. What else can I say? I can't argue with her. Not when I know what she says to be the truth.

"Something else happened to you," she says. "Everything you just told me really did happen — that much is true. But something else happened … *afterward* … but you're not telling me what. Why?"

Why, she asks, but I can't even begin to respond to a question like that. Where *would* I begin?

"Why?"

I sit there on my log, continuing to observe the roughness of my hands. What else can I do? I know what it is she wants from me, but I also know it is the very thing that I will never be able to give in kind. Because she wouldn't understand. I could describe it to her, describe the whole experience in minute detail; but how can I reduce an experience to the description of it? Something always gets lost in the translation. She'll understand it, one day, I know, for sure. But not today. If I could pour the whole of my consciousness, the whole of my being into hers, if only for a moment, she would be there for herself. She would feel. She would understand. But I can't, and so, she won't. In the end, it's beyond her.

"I don't know what happened to me, Allie. I can't explain it. I can't make sense of it to you. I only know that it *does* make sense — more sense than anything else has in my entire life. I *know* that."

"What about your dream last night? You were lying to me about the dream, too. *Why* are you lying to me? You've *never* lied to me!"

"I don't mean to lie — it was never my intention."

"But that's exactly what you're doing!"

"Why tell the truth if you can't understand it?" I say, and even she can't respond to that one. She only stares out at me numbly, her eyes lost, her lips shut. I can see her hands gripping my flask. I can see her hands in the shadows, quivering in dumbfounded fear.

"*What* can't I understand?" she finally asks.

"Can you explain to me the things I can't understand, even if you want me to? How many times have you yourself tried? Can you explain colors to the blind? Can you explain the sunset? The speaker goes dumb and the listener goes deaf."

"I don't believe you," she says, shaking her head faced down toward the dirt. "What could've possibly happened to you that you can't communicate to me? What could *you* possibly know that *I* can't understand?"

I take some time to reply. I feel the anger beginning to simmer up inside of me, deep and bubbling from within, but I take the time to temper it, to maintain my presence as I truly realize what she's actually saying to me.

"*I don't want you to grow past me,*" she's saying to me in the silence. "*I don't want you to leave me back here, alone.*"

"Have you never lied to somebody you've loved?" I finally say. "Have you never lied to somebody because you knew they wouldn't be able to understand the truth?"

Allie continues to stare down at the dirt before raising her trembling eyes to meet mine. She opens her mouth as if to speak, but the words never come. I know what she wants to say, but I know she will never be able to say it. In the end, it doesn't really matter. I understand.

"If there's anybody who can understand me, Allie, you can. If there's anybody who can know and trust me and know that some things can never be explained … it's *you.*"

The silence that encompasses us is engulfing, her face contracted and contorting, her eyes trembling more by the moment. "*Why?*" she finally asks, her question filling the vacuum to imbibe the whole night with meaning. "*Why?*"

"Because I feel it. Because I *know* it."

"This is about last night, then," she says, playing softly with the flask as she looks down at it, away from me. "This is about what you found."

"I don't care about that anymore. I don't care about last night, or yesterday, or the day before that. I don't care about any of it … I care about *you.*"

Allie says nothing for a long time, only continuing to turn that flask over in her hands, over and over again. Her hair drops down in front of her face, but she does nothing to push it away. And then I see her slowly shake her head, but only once, and then she looks up at me quietly, with desperation.

"But why?" she asks. "Why?"

"Because I love you."

Allie stares still at me in the darkness, one last time — one last look of trembling vulnerability before her head droops forward and I hear the flask thud dully in the dirt, and then silence. And when Allie raises up her head again, she is wiping softly away at her tears.

"I'm sorry," she manages out, "I don't know why I'm crying. I *shouldn't* be crying." But then Allie only cries more. I get up and sit next to her on the log and put my arm around her shoulder. Allie puts her arms around me too and continues to cry, her hands light and frail against my chest.

"I don't know how to explain anything," she says, sputtering. "I don't know how to explain, I don't know how to understand, I don't know how to make sense of anything, and I don't know if I'm crazy or sane, but none of it makes any sense, Sean! None of it makes any sense!"

"It's okay," I tell her, stroking her hair. "You don't need to explain it to me. I already understand."

"*How* can you understand?" she asks. "How can you say you understand *anything* when I haven't *told* you anything? And I *haven't* told you anything, Sean! I've *never* told you *anything*, and it…and…" But then Allie just goes quiet and buries her head deep in my chest. "I just want to be good," I hear her whisper. "I just want to be good." I say nothing; I run my hand through her hair and hold her head warm to my chest and comfort her as I can.

"I never lied to you, Sean," she says later. "I never lied to you."

"I know," I say. "I know."

"It was just another symbol," she says, her hands moving across my chest. "Those *things* I bought…I bought them because nothing else made any sense to me…because I'm too messed up and scared and crazy to deal with life in any other way. Because reality is too much for me sometimes; because relationships are too much; because I need protection from it all. Because I need *symbols — structure — narrative —* to make sense of it all. Because nothing else does."

"Everyone needs symbols," I say, watching the embers glow orange in the darkness. "We all need signs to show us the way."

The last sparks of the night crackle up and fly off and away before disappearing entirely. The embers char down from orange to gray, from gray to brown to ashen black. The silence fills our ears; it hums patiently in the void, hissing rhythmically out and through our bodies, bringing unity and closure to us all. She can feel it, I know…I *know* she can feel it.

"Sean…?"

"Allie."

"…I love you."

"I know," I say. "I do."

*   *   *   *   *

I woke up the next morning to the rain falling steadily in my eyes. I woke slowly, as if easing out of a long bath, and looked about at the remnants of the camp. The fire was but a spent, blackened pit, the logs drenched and soaked through. The tent, pitched but never used, was already gone. The flask was wet in the dirt where Allie had dropped it the night before. I picked it up and looked it over, its smooth, cold, stainless-steel feeling funny as I turned it over in my hands. I smirked then, almost kind of smiled, and lobbed it carelessly into the charred remains. I looked around one last time, allowing the down-pouring rain to gather and fall about my hair, to wash cool along the contours of my face. No backpack, no tent, no walking stick. Only the flask remained. It was as I thought, then. Allie had left, long gone, I knew. Allie was long gone to me, and I knew it from the night before.

PART II

Darkness within darkness.
The gateway to all mystery.

– Tao Te Ching

I

Once, when I was very young, I went on a camping trip with a group of friends and their parents. None of them were very close to me, although I think their parents liked me. I was a very well-behaved child, and I think that me being brought along was mostly the parents' doing. I think on some deeper level I knew this, even back then, for the whole trip I did not feel connected to them. I walked behind much of the way, trailing along on my own path, at my own pace. Eventually one of the parents started trailing behind with me. I don't think they liked the idea of one of us being out of sight, way out in the woods like we were, and I don't blame them; by the next morning, I had disappeared.

That morning I had woken up very early, in the cooling light just before the dawn. Dawn is an amazing thing, and it's a shame that so few people ever take the time to witness it. The night plunges into darkness deeper than ever before; you'd never think that dawn was only an hour away. Then the sky turns deep and purple, wide and gigantic like the ocean, and the air buzzes and hums electric in anticipation, and only then do you know something amazing is about to happen — only then do you realize the dawn is only moments away. That morning was like that. I woke up in that cooling, violet light, the air so clear and weightless, and I couldn't just stay there by the camp like I was, couldn't just deny the miracle of all that was happening around me — not just in the air or the sky but in the trees and the grass and the pines, silent and impossible to catch hold of with my hands. Just because I can't explain something doesn't mean it wasn't there—it was inside of me, I felt it, and it made me move—made me leave the camp and explore the woods in search of its own validation. My feet moved of their own accord.

The paths unknown to me, I instead ignored them entirely, walking off through the brush and the undergrowth, between the spaces in the trees. Some time passed, and then I came upon a stream, small and rocky among the ferns. I approached it and bent low beside it to wet my face in the running water. It was very cold, the water in the stream, and when I washed my face with it I could taste the salt and the sweat from all the walking the day before. I sat there for a little while, admiring the sound of the water, watching bubbles rise up and pop between the crevices in the rocks. I've never understood what makes the sound of water so relaxing. The songs of the streams are the songs of their struggles against the stones and the rocks—they always flow along rugged paths. Why should their song be a soothing one? I don't know. I don't know if I ever will.

It still wasn't quite dawn; although I could feel it all around me, its arrival imminent and assured, the sun had not yet come. I looked about me briefly, wondering where I had even gotten to, but fear had not yet taken hold. I knew I was all right. I knew things would be okay, and I knew it from the first moment the hike started—it was only the concerned parents who didn't understand, though I don't blame them for it—even I can't explain what had gotten into me. I'm a very fearful person. There are many decisions I've made in my life that were chosen out of fear, and I'm not proud in saying that. But that day was different. I woke up, and from the moment I awoke, I felt it within me, calling, calling to me in the light in the sky and the hum in the air. I was being summoned, and I was merely responding in kind.

And so I got to my feet again and crossed the stream, balancing myself on the rocks jutting out from the running water. The land picked up steeply after that, up and away toward level terrain from the look of the treetops beyond. I took my time with it, moving deliberately with my hands and feet, holding fast to the tree trunks as they came to me, taking the time to get my footholds before moving on. It was then, making my way up the eroded hillside with my hands in the dirt, that I first heard the voice, singing on in the pre-dawn light, the melody ancient and elemental, emerging as if out of a dream:

Campaka-vane madhura svapane
Ta'ha'ke dekhechi Ma'ya'mukure

I stopped then, if only for a moment, the cool breeze playing through my hair and past my ears, the unknown voice rising to meet me from the top of the hill as if out of the ether:

Sha'nta ba'ta'se madira suva'se
Mugdha nayane sarita'-tiire

I stopped again, an unknowable, volcanic longing erupting up and out from within me, momentous and enveloping, roaring and ecstatic like the sea. I stood straight upon the hillside, my eyes closed, my arms resting by my sides while my young, small heart beat on patiently with the music, the voice leering out to me in rhythmic, teasing waves:

Siitha' kusuma-para'g alakhe a'siya'
Alake bhasiya' ja'y
Setha' maner mayu'r
Niila'ka'she ca'hi kala'pa meliya' dey

I ran up the hillside, plowing up and ahead on all fours at times, unthinking, uncaring, doing anything I could to make it up to the top and to the clearing. There *would* be a clearing, I knew. It was waiting for me.

Only when I reached the top did I finally see her, dancing alone in the clearing that I knew would be there, swirling about in circles with her arms outstretched in the quiet darkness. She was so young, even to my child's eyes. Something about her hair, gold as it was, long and flowing seamlessly with her steps and gestures; she looked barely a day over eighteen.

Jyotsna'-nishiithe vijana viithite
Bha'laba'sa' na'ce ta'ke ghire' ghire'

I stood there quietly for some time, watching her dance — watched as she spiraled out and on in ever-increasing circles — as she stepped and moved and beckoned out with her arms for the dawn's longed-for arrival.

Ta'ha'ke dekhechi Ma'ya'mukure

The last syllable of the girl's song lingered on and drifted away like a fragrance on the breeze. With it, the girl's steps slowed, her circles, her gestures, and soon, she had stopped. The silence pulsed in the darkness; it plunged my ears into a deafening calm. And her hair — her golden hair shimmered in that darkness, as if lit from within.

I heard myself, suddenly. The song gone, I heard my feet shifting in the ground, heard my breathing nervous and unsteady. What was I doing? I found myself wondering, for the first time. Who was this girl, and why was I here?

The girl still had her arms outstretched, as if the dance had continued on in her mind. She had her back to me. If I slipped away, would she hear? The girl's back straightened, straightened, elongated, and arched out so abruptly I thought she might glide away. She went to her knees — straightened her back again and faced east, apparently absorbed in some deep contemplation. This was my moment, I realized. I could turn and run, and she might never know. But would I be able to find my way back?

The girl rose to her feet; she stood and she turned and stared straight on into me.

"Hello," she said, and the fairness of her face opened up to a smile. "How are you?"

"I'm…" Her hair. I couldn't stop staring at her hair. "—I'm lost."

The girl laughed lightly. She looked around at the clearing, as if hearing something, and then turned back to me. "Just in time, then," she said, and started walking over toward me with weightless, peaceful steps.

I grew wary as she approached. "For what?" I asked.

"For what," she repeated, in almost a whisper. She moved across the clearing toward me in an effortless, waif-like gait. She was far, she moved, and then all at once, was close — very close — bending down low to meet my height — her wide, blue eyes matching up to meet mine. And I'll never forget the way she looked at me then, so light and unconditional — knowing and warm like the eyes of my mother — it was almost enough to banish my fears.

"Here," she said, and moved her hands gently to cover my eyes. "Close your eyes."

Darkness. Sound. Movement. Light. "Breathe," she says, and elongates her vowels. "Breeeeathe."

I hear her breath, slow in the space. The wind, carrying on through the trees. Their swaying, graceful and calm in the cool morning breeze.

"Why did you come here?" she whispers deeply in the sound. "Why are you here?"

Her question echoes in my mind as I bring myself back into my past, back as I linger behind my friends' parents along the trails even as we just enter the woods. They look back at me with a worrying and concern that belongs exclusively to adults, and eventually they take turns trailing back behind with me.

"Come along," they say. "We don't want to be left behind." Only, they don't know that I've already moved on without them.

"Where are you?" I hear the girl whisper. "Where are you now?"

I am walking along the path. The parents forget about me sometimes, and when they do I can only stand still and yearning, hearing the call coming to me from between the trees. I wish they would leave me be, so I could be with myself, alone. I wish they would leave me alone, so that I could go and follow the call.

"But why?" she whispers. "Why are you here?"

I woke up and felt the dawn. I woke up and felt the call. I felt the call and followed it, I followed it and came to the river, came to the river and heard you sing, heard you sing and saw you dance, saw you dance and came to be here with you, right now.

"And why are you here?"

To be here, right now.

"With me?"

With you.

"Who am I?"

I am that.

*   *   *   *   *

When I opened my eyes again, it was already light out. The dawn, but an ephemeral show that comes as soon as it goes, was over. The girl seemed unconcerned. Looking into my eyes with her tenderness, with her love, she was stroking her hair and smiling at me; I could feel her hair in the wind against mine.

"It's beautiful," she said, "isn't it?"

"I didn't see it."

She smiled. "But you felt it—didn't you?"

"Yeah." We stood there for some time, saying nothing, and I began to listen to the birds. She was listening, too.

"Birds make great sky-circles of their freedom. How do they learn it?" I didn't know how to respond, so I didn't. "They fall," she said, " —and falling, they're given wings."

"What's that?" I asked, not understanding.

"Rumi."

"What's that?"

"Poetry," she said. "You should learn it, someday." Her eyes began to drift away from mine, finally, looking about at the clearing, at the woods surrounding us on all sides.

"You're really … young," I said, hesitating, not even knowing what I meant.

She smiled. "Younger than you might think."

"What were you singing before?"

"Poetry … I was singing poetry." The girl ran her hand along my cheek, held it there momentarily as if taking it in one last time, and then stood tall on her feet.

"I think you know the way back," she said, but I wasn't sure if she was asking me or telling me. "You do, don't you?"

"I think so. Yes."

"You should go, then. You don't want to worry them."

"But what's your name?"

"Priya," she said, warmly.

"My name's Sean."

"That's good," she said, giving me one last smile before turning to leave.

"But …" I found myself stammering again, watching her back as she left. " —will I ever see you again?"

"Lovers don't finally meet somewhere," she said, still walking away from me. "They're in each other all along."

"But …" I sighed, and knew my sighing wouldn't stop her. " —what does that mean?" I called after her. "I don't understand."

"It's poetry," she said, and turned to face me once more. "You should learn it."

2

I NEVER QUITE THOUGHT IT would ever come to this, and lying there on the wet pavement, my face held up an inch away from a dirty puddle after my last landsliding fall down the muddy trail into the middle of the road, I begin to wonder how I'm ever going to explain this to people. What, exactly, am I supposed to say? That Allie left me alone in the middle of the night on our one-year anniversary? That she left me in the middle of the wilderness, no less, so I had to find my way back alone through the pouring rain? Why does that suddenly sound like some kind of lie?

A thunderclap breaks open the sky and a car lays on its horn and sprays water at me as it drives past. I wipe the mud briefly from my face and rise up against the weakness in my knees before finally getting to my feet. Out in front of me is the road, vandalizing the landscape in an asphalt strip, winding through the mountains and the fog before disappearing through a gorge. The road is Route 214, I know, the gorge Stony Clove Notch. Allie told me about them both before she left. "The one and only crossing with Devil's Path before its eventual terminus at the western end," she had said. "Down suicide chute, across the road, and up past Devil's Tombstone on the other side."

"Why is it called suicide chute?" I had asked at the time.

"Why do you think?"

Having just spent the last two hours mostly falling down it, I no longer have to ask. First I had to trek two miles over the top of Plateau Mountain, an easy hike if it weren't for lightning striking the mountain all about me. After that was the aforementioned chute, a lovely one-mile plunge down two thousand feet of mud, rocks and boulders until finally hitting the notch and the road below.

Across the road, "Devil's Tombstone" is far less foreboding than it sounds, by the look of it just an ordinary campsite. People eye me curiously from their tents as I walk by, perhaps wondering to themselves who this man is, wandering mud covered and alone out on the other side of the chute. Ignoring them, I make my way over to the picnic tables, set closely against a small, mist-shrouded pond. My legs sigh in relief as I sit at the bench and drink the last of the water from the canteen. Rain falls evenly across the pond, thunder echoes distantly across the mountains, and the mist moves stealthily across the surface of the water. The pond showcases the notch in all its gloomy and panoramic glory: on the right, Plateau Mountain descends abruptly out of the dense clouds in a free fall before ascending on my left just as dramatically into the clouds again. Had our trip gone as planned, this would've been our resting point, our lunch break for the day before the ascent up Hunter Mountain, the second-tallest peak in the Catskills. Allie told me there's an old fire tower up there—a looking point from which you can see the whole range. It almost makes me smile, somehow, at the sheer naivety we both had, thinking we could pull this off, pretending as we were, desperately clinging to what we thought was "normal." There will be no more Hunter Mountain for me now—no fire tower and no terminus at the western end. Devil's Path will forever remain unfinished for me, unconquered. Because ultimately, it's not my Path and never was—it's Allie's. I'm on my own journey now. We both are.

3

It's amazing how little the facts can convey the truth sometimes. Sometimes the truth isn't factual; sometimes it's something more. In a way, it's strange for me to remember Priya, dancing for the sunrise. Strange for me because remembering it gives it a kind of validation I've never allowed myself before. I know what happened—I was there. I remember the yearning within me, that morning so many years ago, waking in the camp and feeling the sunrise. I remember leaving the camp out on my own. But I can't remember how it *felt*—or at least not completely. I know that I felt overcome—but what does that word even mean? I can only piece together the experience through snapshots. I remember the way Priya looked, with her long blonde hair. I remember how young she was; I remember the way that she looked into my eyes and the way they shone like spotlights. But what does it mean? I don't know what it means. Are such things heard? And do such things matter? I am here; I am weightless. And in the end, I am left only with representations: blue eyes, blonde hair, spinning circles and graceful dancing. After that, what more is there to do, other than interpret? "This is my story," I can say. "These things happened to me." Only, what good does that do? No matter what may or may not have happened, I will never be able to face the entirety of the thing itself—I am left only to approach it with approximations.

It took me much longer to find my way back to the camp that morning than it took for me to leave it. Stumbling back upon it what felt like a long time later, I found one of the parents standing by the fire pit with his hands on his hips. I don't think he knew that I was gone—his foot was propped on one of the stones by the remnants of the fire, and he wasn't even looking in my direction until he heard me approach from his side.

"Sean?"

I wish I could remember his name. I don't remember his name. I only remember his hands stayed on his hips—that he looked more annoyed than concerned.

"What are you doing out here?"

I probably should have planned some response, I suppose, but I was only a child, and not very cunning. I shrugged. "I dunno."

The man took a deep breath and looked arbitrarily at the sky. His foot was still propped on the stone, his hands still perched on his hips. "Well," he said tiredly, "how long have you been out here?"

How long? The question seemed entirely beside the point. I had just been with Priya, and this man wanted to pin down how much time I had spent.

"I don't know."

The man sighed and finally placed his two feet on the flat ground beneath him. He looked up again at the lightening sky, anything to keep himself from looking at me. "You don't know," he muttered, almost to himself. "You don't know…"

"Wait here," he said, and then walked over to the tent where I knew the parents had slept. When he came back out, he had brought four more parents with him.

"Sean, are you okay?" one of them asked. He crouched down on one knee and had me by the shoulders. He looked into my eyes, and they were nothing like Priya's.

"I'm fine," I said.

"Where did you go?" he asked, and the questions never ended. All these questions—questions that didn't seem to have anything to do with what had just happened to me. They wanted answers, they wanted explanations, concrete facts that would lead to some core truth or understanding, as if there was one. Explanations. Answers. What did they have to do with Priya? How could I explain her to them? How could I explain an experience I didn't even understand myself? Understanding wasn't the point. Eventually I told them what I could: that I woke up early, before the sunrise, and left camp on my own.

"Why?" they asked.

Another shrug. Who knows? I told them that eventually I found a

stream and was washing my face in its water when I heard a woman
sing.
  "You heard a woman singing?"
  Singing.
  "What was she singing?"
  Shrug. Who knows? "Poetry," was what I said, because "poetry"
was what she told me. I told them I climbed up a hill and found a girl
there in a clearing, dancing by herself.
  "A girl?"
  A girl.
  "Dancing?"
  Dancing.
  "How old was she?"
  Who knows? Younger than you might think.
  "So she was young?"
  Younger than you might think.
  The parents began to flash looks of incredulity at each other. The
man who had his hands on his hips before now had his arms crossed,
and I could see him grinning. The parents wanted to know what had
happened next. I told them that she finished her song and finished
her dance; that she closed her eyes and sat silently as I watched.
  Why did I watch?
  Why not?
  What was she doing?
  Nothing.
  Nothing?
  Maybe. I asked them if no-thing was a word, too.
  No-thing?
  No-thing.
  Well what happened next?
  I told them that she opened her eyes and came over to me, too. I told
them that she told me to close my eyes and asked me why I was there.
  Well why was *she* there?
  She just was.
  Well why were *you* there?
  One last shrug. I just was.
  One of the parents, the one who first found me, he took a deep breath
and looked at each of the other parents in turn. Like me, he shrugged.
  The man who was crouched in front of me, holding me by my

shoulders, he held me more gently now. "Sean?" he asked, " —are you sure this wasn't a dream?"

"It felt like a dream."

"Do you think maybe you were sleepwalking?"

I stayed quiet for some time. I had to think about that one. I tried to bring myself back to where I once was — to that *moment* — that moment that had passed and had now turned into memory. It *felt* like a dream. But I *knew* it was real.

"Maybe I was … *dream*-walking."

"Dream-walking," the parent said, and he smirked and then smiled. He looked up at the other parents and they all flashed grins. "That doesn't sound too bad," he said, and he lightly tapped my cheek with his palm. "Let's try to stay awake from now on."

"Why?" I asked, and I really didn't know.

He smiled one last time. "Because you might hurt yourself."

4

I KNEW I WAS SICK all along. It's funny the way your body works sometimes, when it refuses to break down until it can finally afford to. Something clicks, tells your body it's crunch time, and after that it's not allowed to feel sick as you're climbing down a muddy two-thousand foot drop in the pouring rain, as you're hitch-hiking down a remote mountain road. You know it though, deep down. You can feel the sickness even before your body does. I know I did. It's only now, sitting down in the coach bus in Rifton after everything else, completely soaked with my clothes sagging from my skin, only now that my body gives in. It feels the comfort of my cushioned seat, the tempered relaxing in my thighs and legs. "Forget it," my body groans. "I'm done."

Sitting there in my seat, I'm amazed they even let me on the bus. The driver gave me quite a look as he took my ticket, but ultimately a look was all he gave. I kinda feel bad, honestly. My seat will remain wet long after I'm gone.

I cross my arms and close my eyes and try not to think about it, try to wrench my mind from the chills running laps up and down my spine, from the AC vent blowing straight into my soaked and still-dripping face. I realize suddenly that I have a dry change of clothes in my backpack, but realize just as fast that I handed it over to be shoved in the luggage compartment about two minutes ago. Well, it figures. Considering the luck I've had the past two days, I shouldn't have expected much better.

God. Two days. I run them over in my mind. This morning, trekking across the mountaintop, lightning striking the ground all around me.

Last night, holding Allie in my arms, telling her I understood—what, I can't remember. And yesterday. What in God's name happened yesterday? Waking up from that dream, only to spend the day walking through it.

"Hello."

Opening my eyes takes effort, and even after I do it's hard for me to realize just who's greeting me. Those round, staring eyes. That dark, messy hair. And that face, that calm smile. I know that smile. Where do I know that smile?

" …Olivia?"

"Yes," she says, smiling. "Do you mind if I sit here, Sean?"

I murmur out some half response, stumbling over the stuttering of my speech as I realize that it is in fact Olivia who is suddenly on the bus with me. Seeming to ignore my incoherence, Olivia merely thanks me politely and takes her seat. She takes a hemp tote bag from her shoulder, puts it on her lap and begins to rummage through it, apparently looking for something. I watch half in interest, half in numbed-out confusion, my dim, vacuous brain trying to take in that she had come into the restaurant only the day before yesterday—that she had told me I would have to call her soon. Olivia manages to find what she was looking for, some decrepit old hardcover, the sort of thing I'd expect to find under Allie's pillow. Maybe Olivia's reading Tolstoy, too. I eye the cover briefly. *Ten Great Potboilers*, the title reads, by some guy named Max Frank.

"Do you know him?" she asks, catching my curiosity.

"No…I don't read much."

"Neither do I," she says, "but I do like a good mystery." Olivia opens up her book. "Don't you?" she asks, but then turns forward away from me, her eyes staring out at what would be the distance if there wasn't the back of a bus seat in her way. I watch her as she stares forward, her hands palm down upon the pages themselves. I don't answer her. What would be the point, even if she were still with me? I wouldn't even know where to begin answering her question.

Olivia faces me, jerky and all at once.

"You know what I like about mysteries?" she asks, but I don't respond. "That they always give you *answers*. Maybe not the answers you expected, or even the ones you want, but there's always an answer in the end." She seems immensely pleased by this, and even starts to grin. "Maybe that's why they call them escapist!"

The bus closes its door and finally pulls away from the curb. Sitting in the seat next to me, Olivia has gone back to facing forward, her hands palm down upon the pages. I struggle to bring my mind back to the present, to snap it out of its sickness and deal with the business at hand. It won't be long now. The ride home from Rifton isn't far, even in this weather. I've got twenty minutes, tops. Twenty minutes to distract Olivia from whatever it is she's doing and finally get some answers. "How did you *know*?" I want to ask. But knowing is a funny word, a funny concept altogether. How did I know Allie would leave me? How did I spend a year trying to know her, failed, and then suddenly understood her in the blink of an eye? And why does that knowledge only come in flashes? Why does it never sustain itself or last for anything more than mere moments? I don't know. Because I *did* know, last night, holding Allie in my arms. I knew it all, knew her secrets and her ways—I *felt* it last night, felt it all in a flash. I *know* I did—so why do I know no longer? "Knowledge is just a point of view," Allie once told me, but I have no idea what in the hell that even means.

Olivia is still looking ahead into the imagined distance, now turning the page of her book, apparently looking for new passages to palm before remaining still once more.

Is this all a distraction, though? What could Olivia possibly know that could help me now? Who *can* help me now? Allie didn't have any friends, or at least not any she introduced me to. I bring my mind back and try to think of somebody who Allie might have told me about, some old friend maybe, some ex-boyfriend, somebody close to her whom I might be able to talk to, but I know the effort is fruitless even before I begin—the very idea of Allie having some ex-boyfriend is a bad joke, much less old friends. She seems unreal to me now, without substance, amorphous and ephemeral like the mist. Like a ghost—some ectoplasmic hallucination that materialized into my life one night and materialized out of it another.

The night we first met: she was drunk, was what she said. Was drunk and stumbling and hardly knew where she was, although for some reason she was completely sober only a few minutes later when I told her how Lily had dumped me. That was such a strange night. I can hardly understand it, even now. I had just come across Lily in the bar, drunk and dancing with her friends. I was so angry when I left that bar, but even my anger was just a front for how sad and broken-hearted I really was. Then all of a sudden there was Allie, this gorgeous girl I had never even seen before, there in front of me, wanting a ride home. How is it possible? How *could* it be possible? She was perfect—perfect hair, perfect smile, perfect body, perfect everything—this perfect being who manifested out of the shadows all at once to take me and change my whole perception—a being with no past, no history, no life and no friends—and now suddenly I was with her. It doesn't add up. It just doesn't make any sense, and this time it's not just my insecurities talking. I'm missing something, I realize, some vital part of the equation. There's something else I need to know.

Or at least I think there is.

Olivia begins humming to herself, some pleasant tune I've never heard before. I turn to look, and she's bobbing her head to some self-constructed beat, her hands still palming the pages. What in God's name is she doing? Do I attract people like this into my life, or do I just imagine them? Olivia begins tapping her fingers on the pages, her fingers moving to the beat with her head.

Whether I like it or not, this is my life, even if it does feel like a dream; and no matter how uncanny she seems to me now, I *remember* Allie, remember Allie with her arm around me, for some reason pretending to be drunk on the night we first met. Allie—on the railway trestle with me, with the father who had leaped from the bridge—taking me into the abandoned mining caves in High Falls—deep, to an underground lake—turning off the flashlight and telling me, "be still." Allie, and Shaft 2A, her "best kept secret"—hidden streams and waterfalls, waterholes—unmaintained, backwoods paths to Lake Awosting; and Allie—holding my hand for the first time—leading me through wildflowers down to helipads—her lips, against mine—my hands, running through her hair; her shampoo—her face—her hand, in mine, rougher than you might expect—calluses, from doing what, I'll never know; Allie, walking in through the back door of my house, right off the rail trail—the smell of grass, of freshly cut wood—wildflowers, in her hands, just picked by the riverside. "Smell them," she says. I do, and they smell wonderful. Allie smiles. Allie smiles and kisses me on the cheek; she buys condoms she never intends on using—roams the woods at night, alone, eyeing strangers and thinking of me. Allie sits with me in her room, and we listen to Bach. Her eyes flutter back and close—her hands move delicately in the air.

"Counterpoint," she says — the sublimity to be found in disciplined emotion — in subtle, tempered systems and forms. Polyphonic voices climax in a fugal frenzy, Apollo reconciles itself with the primordial latency of Dionysus, but I don't understand; I never do understand, and even when I do, it's too late. It's always too late. "Can you hear it?" she says, and her hands are high in the air. "Can you *hear* it?"

"Where is she?" I blurt out. "Just … tell me where she is."

Olivia blinks spasmodically and turns to face me as if she didn't know I was there. "I'm sorry, what?"

"You have to know where she is," I say, my voice whispering in hoarse sputters. "You have to."

"Who?"

"Allie!"

"Allie … Allie … I know an Allie … "

"Allie *Donowitz* — my *girlfriend*, remember? You came into my restaurant the day before yesterday. You said I'd need to talk to you — you said I'd need to talk to you about *this*. You *knew* what was going to happen."

"Ohhh, I remember now," she says, sounding pleased. "Allie Donowitz. I like Allie."

"But, you *knew* — you *knew* what was going to happen … "

"Knew what was going to happen?"

"You told me that I'd need to talk to you about her."

"Why would you need to talk to me about Allie?"

"Because … Because … But you *told* me I'd need to talk to you … "

"Well, yeah. You will need to talk to me. Not about Allie though." Olivia takes the time to close her book, her hands running over its worn cover before she looks up at me and smiles with an understanding I'm not sure she understands herself.

"Why?" she asks sweetly. "Is something wrong?"

I look into Olivia's eyes. Her dumb, staring eyes. Those eyes that so closely resembled spotlights when I first looked into them, only two days before. Maybe something has changed. Maybe something has changed in me. But I look at them now and see nothing — nothing.

"No," I eventually croak, and sit back in my seat. "Everything's cool. Things are just awesome."

"That's good," Olivia says, her blind warmth never leaving her, "but I still think you will have to call me soon, you know."

"Oh?" I ask, but I'm looking away, and no longer care.

"Yes, but don't worry about it."

"Don't worry," I say, staring out through the window, out at the rain, "I won't."

*   *   *   *   *

I don't remember much of the rest of the ride. Maybe I cried, but I don't think so. I think it was just all the rain, still dripping from my hair, the sweat on my face salty like tears. I don't know what I was feeling. I walked off the bus in a sick, semi-delirious daze, stumbling down Main Street, eventually down Water Street, rain sloshing in my socks. When I got home I dropped my backpack in the driveway, walked around the house and came upon the river flowing on behind it, fresh like a revelation. I don't know why I went back there that day, why it was that I had to see the river, to validate its existence. I was so sick, already so much sicker than I had been on the bus—I hardly knew where I was, much less what I was doing.

The rain was just clearing up then, I remember. I sat on a log by the water's edge—the same log I had sat on only two days before with Ivan. I sat and watched the clouds break, watched the sun set dim and blaring through it all, mist drifting up from the flood plains across the river like smoke from a dying fire. I sat there for a long time, numb and paralyzed, the sickness creeping through me, coursing through my head and pounding in my brain, my heart pumping thick in my ears until it was all I could hear. I think I might have actually cried then, a few tears escaping from my eyes before I finally crouched over, held my head in my hands and waited for the spinning sickness to pass, for the nightmare to be over. When I finally looked up again, I knew I could go inside. When I finally got inside, Ivan was sitting in the living room, waiting for me.

"Vanya…" I groaned, but he silenced me altogether.

"You are sick," he said, and looked me over seriously. "I will take care of you."

5

I DESCEND DEEP THAT NIGHT; I leave my mind behind. I am sitting on a ragged, worn-out couch, stained yellow where once it was white. I am facing a television. Something is on, but all I make out are dim, populated forms—out-of-focus, meaningless. Allie is sitting with me. I feel my arm around her, but feel little else. We have just come back to the apartment—our apartment. We spent the night out on the town; we ate Thai cuisine. Allie likes Thai food. Allie likes just about all foreign food. Thai, Ethiopian, Sushi and even Indian, but I don't complain. We ate and laughed together and later we walked the windy sidewalks and Allie kissed me, without reason, without warning. Why complain?

"I want to go to Venice," Allie says, drinking her white wine. Venice. The word strikes me. I don't remember Allie ever wanting to go to Venice before. I don't remember Allie ever even leaving the valley. "The pictures look so beautiful," she says. "I want to go to Venice and see something so beautiful."

"We should go," I say. "We can save up the money, if we just take the time. We can go together."

"Beauty," she says. "Beauty for its own sake. Maybe I'll go to France. Go live in Burgundy and experience some *real* culture."

"I don't speak French. I hear they don't like Americans."

"If I had the money to go to France, I'd leave tomorrow. There's nothing keeping me here. I'd go. I'd go tomorrow."

My arm is still around her. I remove it so I can drink my wine, too. I don't know what kind it is, but the taste is bad and bitter in my mouth. I don't remember when we bought this. I don't remember when Allie drank wine to begin with.

"Why?" Allie asks. "Where would you go?"

"I don't know," I say, bending forward on the couch, the noise from the TV buzzing dully in the background. "Mongolia, maybe. Morocco."

"Hah!" she laughs. "Morocco."

We sit there quietly for some time, both of us staring at nothing, not even at the TV. Then I hear Allie sigh and the next thing I know she is leaning her head on my shoulder, sighing. Taking the cue, I put my arm around her again and pet at her hair, although we still aren't talking. I sit there and think about the things she said. I sit there and think about France and Burgundy and wonder if it is anywhere near Bavaria. Wonder what I will do when she leaves. Wonder if there is any place out there for me at all.

"I'm tired," she says, still leaning quietly on my shoulder. "Thanks for dinner."

"My pleasure."

"Wine always makes me sleepy," she says, although I can't recall a time that Allie ever drank wine before. "I'm so tired." Wasn't there some anniversary? Some anniversary by the fireside? But I can't make sense of it. Can't make sense, can't remember, can't recall. Nothing makes sense and nothing garners recollection.

Allie gets up and goes to the bathroom to change, although I don't understand why she takes the time to change into clothes she knows she's going to take off in a few minutes anyway. Is it deliberate? I don't know. Maybe I'm just a good kisser.

I wait on the bed for some time. Allie comes into the room later, fresh from her change, braless in a tank top and yoga pants. "I'm so tired," she says, cuddling up next to me on the bed, giving me a kiss. "I'm always so, so tired."

"I know," I say, kissing her back, my hand running warm underneath her top. "So am I."

When it's all over we lie quietly in the darkness and listen for the white noise outside the windows, for the dogs and the neighbors and the distant sirens, but there are none; no noise to fill the void, but only the dense silence in its stead. I pet at Allie's hair and wonder at the silence, think about it and wonder what it means, but then Allie's laughing. Allie's laugh was so sudden in that silence. It was loud like a witch's cackle.

"What?" I ask. "What are you laughing at?"
"Nothing," she says. "I'm laughing at nothing."

*   *   *   *   *

I woke up after that, slept again, and the cycle went on perpetually
from there. I'd open my bleary eyes hot in the summer heat; I'd feel
the sweat coating my skin, warm and membranous like placenta,
other times sticking cold to me, moist and gelatinous like a tomb. I'd
fall back into my sleep again after that, emerge once more. I'd wake
and watch the ceiling lift back and peel off, watch it expose me to the
shimmering, incomprehensible light of the stars above, other times
wake to watch the fire burn from the hearth like a hell pit, watch
as it'd catch on the ancient, peeling wallpaper and burn the whole
house down around me, down to its skeletal remains. Sometimes I'd
wake and see Ivan there too, watching me, leaving me hot water, the
occasional soup, although I don't remember eating any. I remember
shivering, wrapped in blankets, sputtering nonsense to the world; feeling alone and empty—an alienated, isolated soul wandering lost in
a vast, uncaring universe. I watched the sun beat in focused through
my porthole window, imagined its fire spew out embryonic planets
from its womb, imagined the earth mature and decay, imagined the
sun consume it once more, a red giant reclaiming what was once
hers—my blind, unthinking, ultimately just and ever-righteous
God. And then I'd wake and see Ivan again, as though he never left.
"Ivan..." I'd moan without meaning.
"Yes, yes," he'd say, but I'd only moan over again.
"Take a message. Be sure to write it down..."
"Yes, yes," he'd say. "Yes, yes."
Time passed but never seemed to, the way oil when poured moves
but never looks it. It all continued, repetitive and unending, trapped
along my sickening Möbius strip, until one day I awoke; one day, I
returned.

*   *   *   *   *

Ivan sits by the foot of the bed patiently, his hands in his lap, his eyes
quietly trained on me, wrapped as I am in the blankets on the bed.
"You are awake then," he says. "Actually awake, I mean."

I don't reply right away, and instead try unraveling myself from the mass of blankets all about me. "It's so hot," I say.

"Yes." Ivan gets up from his chair by the bedside and hands me a glass of water from which I gladly drink.

"I suppose turning on the AC wouldn't have been the best idea," I concede.

"You were very sick," he says, shaking his head, drinking from his own glass. "You slept two days."

"Two days," I say, staring out at the light coming in through my porthole window. The day I first met Olivia in the restaurant, Allie left me the very next night. That was two days. These were two more.

My God. How is such a thing possible?

"Yesterday you awoke for a short time," he says, crossing his legs. "You kept telling me to take a message. In case somebody were to call, I suppose."

"Did anyone call?"

"No."

"No," I repeat back, facing the window again, sighing. "No . . ."

I almost expect Ivan to say something then, to ask me what happened, but he already knows, and I knew it already. Silence descends, thick and humid and undeniable. I look back to him, expecting to see his eyes on me, but he only looks away at the ashen fireplace, used up firewood still left over in its pit from the night Allie stayed over, only three days before. He does know, then. For once, he doesn't have to tell me.

"She left me, Ivan," I let out, " — left me in the middle of the woods."

Ivan doesn't look at me but only continues to eye the fireplace, nodding very slowly, a quiet breath escaping through his nostrils.

"You don't look very surprised," I say.

Ivan shakes his head. "I am sorry," he says. "Very sorry."

Nothing more is said. I come out partially from underneath my blankets and allow my skin to bathe in the fresh air; I drink from my water and feel its moisture cool me from within. Ivan is looking at the fireplace, his eyes sometimes closed, other times open, his gaze never leaving. Sometimes he lets his hands rest in his lap, other times he rubs at his chin and runs his fingers through his beard. It's not for another minute or so that he finally speaks again.

"She loves you, you know." He looks up at me in meaning. "You do know that?"

I already see where this is going. I don't know why he insists on being this way, really. I don't understand why he won't just let me be, let me do my own thing without his rational eye piercing my every move.

"Yes." I look absently out at the window.

"You intend on looking for her," he says, and I only look back at him with a sidelong glance. "Yes?"

I feel like lying to him then, lying to him out of sheer spite. He would see the lie for what it is, of course, but at least he'd know how spiteful it was. I want to lie out of spite just so he can feel my spite. But eventually I just relent and concede to him anyway. In the end, it's not worth the effort. "Yes," I tell him, "I intend on looking for her."

Ivan gets up abruptly from his chair. "Sean, listen to me. Allie loves you. Do you understand? She has *always* loved you. But you need to *trust* her. You *must* trust her!"

I look at him, scowling, and measure my words with precision. "Allie just left me," I say, "alone in the goddamn wilderness in the middle of the goddamn night so I could wander back, sick and alone through the pouring goddamn rain."

Ivan raises his eyebrows and very nearly rolls his eyes. "Is that a fact?"

"I deserve to know what the hell is going on. I deserve to know the truth."

"You already do. You *know* you do. But now you are confused. You are angry, hurt, lonely … I understand that. But trying to hunt her down, Sean, to find her only so you can strangle meaningless facts out of her for your own self-satisfaction, your own gratification — does that sound like love to you?"

"And what *does* sound like love, Ivan? Because I'm just curious! Leaving me in the middle of the night the moment things get too real? The moment things get too *honest*?"

"You cannot even convince yourself that that is what happened, much less me, Sean. You can spin the facts all you want, but they still add up to lies."

"Nobody cares about me! Nobody! Not one fucking person!"

"Are you really going to try to pretend that you are actually surprised by any of this? How many months have I listened to you elaborate this drama to me? How many months have you gone on with it, trying to pretend it was all okay, no matter what you heard from me?"

"Yeah, you're right," I seethe, lying back on the bed. "I should've seen this coming. A million miles away. How stupid of me! Of *course* I should've expected her to leave me alone in the middle of the mountains. Don't know how I missed that one."

Ivan sits back in his chair then, crosses his arms and glowers at me. I know what he's thinking. He wants to dare me to do it. *You know where she lives*, he wants to say to me. *Why not drop by?* Because he knows where she lives, too. Not at Lenape Hall on campus anymore, but at the Orphanage, set back on the border against the woods. And he knows I'll find nothing there, just as well as I know it. And he knows it will do no good, as do I. But I *have* to do it—and even Ivan knows that I must.

"You do realize that there is no rationality in this," he says, " —yes?"

"Yes."

"What could you possibly hope to find?"

"The truth."

"The truth? The *truth*, Sean, is that Allie is a confused and disturbed individual. That she has no emotional right to be in *any* relationship, much less one with you. Maybe she finally realized that for herself—maybe she finally woke up to it. Maybe she needs to be on her own, Sean. You cannot help her—*that* is the truth."

"No it's not. That's *not* the truth."

Ivan leans back in his chair and continues to cross his arms. He smiles then, and I can hardly believe it myself. He smiles and uncrosses his arms and runs his hands through his long, black hair.

"Which part, exactly?" he asks, and his words hang suspended in the air. "Which part?"

6

IF THERE'S ONE PLACE in town that Allie would go, where would it be? I ask myself the question continually. I am standing outside my house, in the middle of the road, and I don't even know which direction to start with. I look to the left. Fifty yards down, there is another house, and then more houses soon. Only a quarter mile down or so, and the road leads back to town—to Main Street—to it all. I look to the right. The road is empty. Fifty yards down, the road winds off to the right, crosses the river and leaves town. I look straight ahead across from my house. Woods. Trees. Somewhere in there, my campus. I look behind. My house. The rail trail. The river.

If there is one place that Allie would go, where would it be? The woods? "This is where I am," she once told me. "This is where I'm from."

But it's *not* where she's from, as much as she'd like me to think it. I *know* where Allie is from. Allie's from town, just like everyone else. She grew up in a house, just like everyone else—and I know where that house is—I can locate it upon the earth and point to it with my finger. Allie's not from the woods; Allie is from a decrepit old Victorian, just like half the people in this town. Somewhere, deep down, Allie knows this; somewhere, deep down, Allie fights it. I picture Allie's mother, looking down at me from the tall, gabled windows: her long hair unfurling in curls, down past her shoulders, her hand upraised to greet my arrival. Allie wouldn't go there, would she? Allie's mother knew; Allie's mother *knew*.

I look to the left again. I look down the road, at the house in the distance and the houses beyond that. Allie could be in any one of them; but if there is one thing I *do* know, it's that Allie wouldn't take roads—even if she were walking from this place to that. Allie would go through the trees; Allie would go through the woods.

"Where are you going?" I turn to look, and Ivan's standing in the open doorway behind me. If I didn't know any better, I'd say he looked concerned. "Are you going to the Orphanage?"

"What do you care?"

Ivan continues to look at me, and doesn't say a word.

"I'm going for a walk," I say. "Want to come?"

"A walk…" Ivan repeats, and takes a few measured steps forward outside. He appears to not want to venture out completely; he wants to only meet me halfway. "Are you not working tonight?" he asks.

"Not for another hour. Come on, I'm just going for a walk through the woods into town. We could get a cup of coffee afterward."

Ivan stands there silently and crosses his arms.

"My treat?"

"I think I will pass," he finally says. I stand there, looking back at him. For some reason, some vague reason I can't even understand myself, I'm fairly surprised. I almost feel like arguing with him.

"Okay … I guess you'll see me later then."

Ivan stands outside the house, stiffly, nods, and doesn't take even one step further. He continues to regard me from the door. "I will," he says. "Or, maybe you will see me, too."

Ivan turns back around to leave me behind.

*   *   *   *   *

Sometimes it's difficult to remember my life in this town before Allie—before Lily, even. Sometimes it's difficult to remember my life in this town before the woods—back to a time when I had yet to have entered them. My freshman semester was similar to most people's, I suppose. I was drunk much of the time—nervous, excited—as awkward as everyone else. Vanya was there for me, in those times. Vanya was my roommate during my very first semester, and of all the people I have met here in this town over the years, he was the very first one.

The first few weeks passed without much meaning. Ivan and I

introduced ourselves to one another, set up our lives on opposite sides of the room and didn't interact very much at all. Ivan is quiet much of the time, silent, and often disapproving. He never drank, never smoked, and never appeared to care when I did. I got the sense that he didn't like me, and began to wonder what he did with his nights — Ivan would usually come home as late as me, but as sober as the day he'd been born.

"This town is very beautiful," he once said, "once you get to know it." We were in our room that night, early in our first semester. We had just walked in, and both at the same time. He was sitting on his bed, on the opposite side of the room, and a part of him was still gazing at the darkness in the window.

"What, so you just walk around town all night?" The idea seemed foreign to me — I had spent the better part of the night hanging out in a room down the hall, flirting with a girl who was kind enough to explain to me the emotional significance of a tattoo on her thigh. At the time, I had hardly even left the campus borders, much less made my way into town. I heard the walkways through the woods were difficult to navigate at night; our college officially discouraged it.

"There is much more here than simply just a town."

"What is there?" I asked, and thought of the thigh tattoos I might have been missing.

Ivan smiled. I'll never forget the way he smiled. "There are woods," he said. "There are trees."

It was so strange, the lilt of his voice as he spoke when he did. "Woods." "Trees." Words so simple, and yet they hummed and pulsed with mystery and meaning. Before then, I had only thought of the woods as obstacles to walk through, but Ivan spoke of them as if they were entities all their own. I wished he would have told me more; I might have listened.

A number of weeks passed, and not much changed. I look back on those times, those early days, and wonder what Allie might have been doing. It was summer, and I know she lived on campus that first year, away from her home — so nearby — away from her mother. Allie lived in a single, once I first met her, but things must have been different that first year, because all freshmen are categorically assigned to live in doubles. *Doubles.* The thought seems incredibly bizarre to me: Allie in a double, with a roommate, or stranger yet, in a suite; Allie, living in a five-person suite — sharing a room with another freshman, just

as new as me, as nervous, as excited, as awkward as everyone else;
Allie, sharing a suite with four other girls, talking about boys, getting
drunk at parties and bringing back boys; *Allie*; to share a space with
Allie, even when I never could.

I don't know what Allie did during that time. She certainly never
spoke to me about it; about the most Allie ever told me about her
past was that it involved camping periodically with daddy. I hardly
even know what Ivan did that first year. For my own part, I spent
most of my time in my dormitory hall, drinking in rooms and going
to parties. Set back on the edge of campus, my hall was exclusively
freshmen; and it's hard to believe now, that they would group us all
together in one building — kids just out of high school, as young
and as stupid as me. But I met Steve then, in those days: Steve, who
later introduced me to the restaurant I would one day work at; Steve,
at whose house I would someday meet Lily. Funny to think of it.
Steve was assigned to my floor by the providential grace of random
chance alone. Had I not met him, I would never have met Lily; had
I not met her, I would never have met Allie. Chains of events often
start haphazardly — you never know where a path will lead you.
Mine started in that dorm, on that floor, with Steve, often drunk.
Steve and I used to drink, used to smoke, used to run around outside
screaming and shouting at nothing, our hands up in the air, holding
bottles of beer, announcing our newfound freedom to the world. As
ridiculous as it was, it led me down a path that one day brought me
to Allie — but Ivan was removed from it all. I imagine Allie would
have been, too.

But then things changed one night. For the first few weeks Ivan
and I lived our separate lives on our respective sides of the cramped
little room and hardly spoke at all, and then one night Ivan — for
whatever reason — decided it was time. It was late that night — a
school night even — and I had been asleep; Ivan had to shake me
before I finally awoke.

"Sean!" he whispered, nudging at my shoulder. "Wake up!"

"What?" I asked, stirring. "What's going on?" I was almost scared.
Ivan and I weren't friends; waking me up in the middle of the night,
I could only assume that something was wrong. But standing over
me — quietly, entirely calm — Ivan didn't even reply at first, but
only stood there, almost smiling. It was cool that night — late in
the summer — and I could feel it as I awoke in the air in the room.

Moonlight shone on his hair from the window. I could see his smile, even in that moonlight.

"Put on a light jacket," he said. "I want to show you something."

I said nothing, but only looked back up at him. He was so composed, standing there over me. It was hard for me to get over the weirdness of it all.

"Dude, what the hell," I finally said, rubbing my eyes, forcing myself to at least try acting normal, "—what time is it?"

"It is late," he replied. "And it is time to go."

I sighed and sat up in my bed, barely aware of where I even was. "Where?" I asked.

But Vanya merely smiled. "Trust me."

Ivan left me alone then, without warning, without explanation, and I was left to myself—to lie in my bed and wonder what he wanted. I lay there—bewildered, confused—asking myself what on earth this creepy foreign kid I hardly knew could possibly want from me, and almost went back to sleep. It's hard to say what happened next. I was ready to write him off; in a way, over the preceding weeks I already had. But lying there—witnessing the moonlight, listening to the crickets, feeling the freshness of the air—something else happened, and something I didn't expect: I got up; I followed him.

It's hard to explain things you can hardly explain to yourself. I don't know why we feel the need to pin everything down to some centrality. The world is more open than we might like, maybe. Sometimes you act without thinking; sometimes you reach without seeing; and a few moments after Ivan left me, I found myself stumbling down the stairs, shaking off sleep, following where he had gone. He had left me lying in bed, and without an explanation for me to cling to; he left me with nothing, perhaps, except for an implicit trust in me that I would follow—and if anyone's surprised that I did, it's me.

When I reached the bottom of the stairs I was hesitant, even, to open the doors, feeling as if at the entrance of a grand, archaic temple. I took a deep breath and pushed my weight behind it, feeling the door struggle to keep me inside. I felt the cool night air enter and envelop me, even before I could see it—could feel it frisk and curl and move about my feet. I felt the weight of the door give way as it held itself open, and standing back, I stayed in the threshold and beheld the world set out before me: at fog, buoyed low upon the earth; at mist, painting the black night gray; and Ivan, standing in the midst of it all; Vanya — standing as he was beneath the lamppost down the way.

Ivan smiled as he saw me — smiled as he had earlier in the moonlight; and as I approached, I knew he would speak. "Do you know what Shawangunk means in its original language?" Ivan was enclosed in a breadth of fogged light within the reach of the lamppost; his breath was settling loosely in the air.

"What's 'Shawangunk'?" I asked, and nearly whispered.

"The name," he said, motioning with his head, "of the ridge that overlooks the town." I looked where he motioned and saw only fog.

"I thought it was called the Mohonk. The Mohonk Mountain."

"Mohonk is the name of the particular part of the ridge they built a hotel on. The name of the whole ridge, the entire mountain whose shadow we are in, actually that is the Shawangunk. The Shawangunk Ridge."

"What does it mean?"

"You know, most of the old names around here are Dutch, or French, or German. Catskill, Plattekill, Wallkill … Shawangunk is different. Shawangunk is native to this place — a part of it — it is indigenous."

"What does it mean?"

Vanya smiled once more. "'In the smoky air.'"

Ivan looked out at the nothing of the night beyond the lamppost and motioned again with his head. "The path goes this way," he said, staring off into the enshrouded, stilling darkness. "I have something to show you."

The dormitory hall was on the far edge of campus, further away from town than any other hall. Walking out the front door, there was only one lit pathway that led to the rest of campus, down past a pond before reaching the other dorms. Ivan, of course, wasn't taking me down a lit pathway to campus at all; walking away from the lamppost, past the last marker of sight we had, Ivan was taking me around the hall, around the back — the back, where there were only woods. Walking further away from the lone lamppost, I began to get nervous. How would we see where we were going? I looked up at the dormitory hall looking down at us six stories from above — the last few lights left on in the late night breathed smoky light out like dim lanterns and then faded out in the fog. Up ahead, I could barely make Ivan out, continuing to walk along the side of the building, and all I could do was follow behind.

Ivan stopped in his tracks and waited for me to catch up. When I did, he looked at me with his head cocked, almost with curiosity. "I suppose you cannot see where we are going," he said.

"What—you can?"

"Well," he said, "look down." When I did, I saw that we were on gravel—a small gravel path that eventually led away from the building and into the trees in the distance.

"What is it?" I asked. "Aren't there just woods out there?"

Ivan looked to where I looked, and I thought I saw him smile. "It's a service road, I believe…" He went quiet for a moment before catching me with a sidelong glance. "But it goes somewhere…special."

"Special? …What does that mean exactly?"

But Ivan was already leaving me behind. "Dammit," I muttered, and followed him back a safe distance behind.

Convinced that we'd never be able to see our way at all, I paid attention to my feet as I walked, taking comfort in the crunch of the gravel, thinking that as long as I could hear the gravel beneath me, I'd still at least be on the right path. So I walked, and walked, and the further I walked…the brighter things got. Confused, I looked behind where we had started, back at the lamppost. The world looked empty out there. The light was a lone beacon, beaming out like an echo in the vacuum of the night. And yet all around me there was light, filtered gray through the fog, twinkling in the moisture, the darkness nearly shimmering. I had to stop, and stand, and turn round panoramically to convince myself I wasn't imagining it: the sparkling darkness.

"Ivan," I finally said, stopping in the gravel, looking at the wall of gray all around me. Ivan stopped too. "—what the hell is this?"

"What do you mean?"

"What do you mean, 'what do you mean'? Will you look at this? I can see everything, and there's not even any light!"

Ivan looked all around us and finally smiled, faintly, as if having expected it all along.

"The moon is out tonight," he said, looking up in the sky, perhaps at where the moon might have been. "The fog has a special love for the moon, Sean, a very special love. The fog makes the moon a part of herself—she imbibes it, distills it in the air and illuminates the path, no matter how far from light we may be."

"So you're telling me we could be out in the middle of the woods and we'd still be able to see?"

"The fog allows you to only see where you yourself are, and not up ahead and not back behind." Ivan seemed immensely pleased. "And so, actually you must live in the present."

"The present?" Ivan was already walking away. "Right," I said, now to myself. "Sure."

Left on my own, I looked out at the building we were leaving behind—the building that over the last few weeks I had grown to consider my home. Blanketed and concealed in the fog, I could no longer make out the building at all, but only its sparsely scattered still-lit windows, glowing pale and orange like lights within ruins. Did it always look this way, even when I wasn't there to witness it? How many nights like this one had passed already without my knowledge, with me, drunk, passed out in a corner I considered my room? I looked back ahead where Ivan had gone, into the enclosed dome of shifting, gray, incandescent darkness. Making my first step forward again, I heard my foot settle quietly in the gravel beneath me. "Follow the gravel," I told myself, watching the fog move briskly through the pines. If I followed the gravel, I'd be on the right path.

Walking down the path, through the trees and into the forest, I was suddenly shocked by the absence of all things that seemed to make sound. I'd walk, and stop, and standing there, I would hear … nothing—and nothing is louder than you might think. Like the lone lamppost, set there in the night only to call attention to the night's own darkness, so too do solitary sounds echo endlessly in the encompassing wake of soundless, empty spaces. Breaking the silence, I would breathe deep, exaggerated breaths through my mouth and watch the air smoke out in front of me; but with Ivan long gone, the lights long gone, the campus a world away, there were no sounds save the sound of my self.

Time passed. At first the path followed grass and then, several minutes later, wound to the left through a parting of trees. I expected to hear the sounds of animals, of insects, of all the hallmarks of cool summer nights, but continued to hear—nothing. "Nothing comes of nothing," Allie once told me, and I quote her here as she often quotes others. " —Speak again!"

The trees giving way once more to grass, I expected to finally come upon Ivan, but neither heard nor saw any trace of his presence. I breathed heavily in the silence and treaded the gravel in nearly a tiptoe.

"Ivan," I said, mustering a voice as normal as I could. "Are you there?"

My voice vandalized the landscape like a sheer act of trespassing. I turned in a circle and saw only fog.

"Ivan," I whispered, as lightly as my steps. "Ivan."

Turning in the gravel, I heard wind gust at my ears like a rejection from the earth itself. Sound enveloped me, mocking me in its power, laughing at my lightness, and turning, turning, with the foggy darkness closing in on me from all directions, suddenly — the wind stopped.

"Ivan?" Appearing from the air, not ten feet from where I stood, Ivan was standing there all at once. He stood with his back to me, and looked out at the silence as if it would speak.

"Ivan!" He didn't turn to acknowledge me. "Jesus Christ," I said, rushing ahead to stand by his side. "I thought I lost you." Ivan still didn't turn, but looked at me with his eyes, a faint smile playing upon his lips. "Dude — where are we going?"

"We are already here," he said.

"What?" I tried to keep myself from panting. Apparently, I had run over to him faster than I realized. " — where?"

"Here."

I looked around and saw only the same wide wall of gray I had seen before. Ivan kept walking.

"Ivan!" I whispered, but he still didn't stop. I ran after him. The ground beneath us turned abruptly from gravel to mowed grass, and only then did Ivan stop.

"Dude — where are we?"

Ivan didn't even cast a glance in my direction but only continued to look out at the thick air beyond. He crouched down low and took off his shoes.

"Why are you taking off your shoes?"

"Because I want to."

"Should I take off my shoes?"

"If you want to." He walked ahead into the grass and left his shoes behind.

"Dammit," I muttered under my breath, and threw my shoes off too. "Wait up!" I said, and ran ahead to follow him.

The grass was cool and wet beneath my bare feet, and I could hear my steps slop as I walked. I had lost sight of Ivan, and spun round in circles. There was darkness all around me, and I couldn't even see where I was.

"Ivan!"

Plop slop plop, I heard, off in the distance. *Plop slop plop.*

"Ivan!"

The grass stuck wet to my ankles and tickled the spaces between my toes. I breathed hard from running and saw nothing but the smoking of my breath from my nostrils.

Plop slop plop, I heard. *Plop slop plop.* And standing there, afraid to even move a muscle, Ivan emerged out within my line of vision like a vision from a dream.

"Jesus Christ," I said, sighing in relief. "Where the hell were you, man?"

"Nowhere." Ivan looked at me up and down, as if suddenly realizing that I had misinterpreted something. "Come," he said, "let us sit."

We sat there a long time that night. Longer, perhaps, than I can even remember. But sitting there, alone in the fog with Ivan, he spoke to me — really spoke to me — for the first time since we had met: of America; of the town and the valley; of his old home in Russia. He had grown up in the Urals, he told me: "The straddling borderland of the east and the west.

"It is neither here nor there," he said. "The last arm of Asia in its groping toward Europe."

"What do you mean?" I played with the grass, light in my hands.

"It is a place between places," he said, and looked at the nothing out beyond. "Russia has always been removed from Europe, in a way. For hundreds of years, Europe looked to us as a barbaric outpost — hardly Europe but not quite justifiably Asia. Russia is a cold place — an open place, a beautiful place; it is interstitial. You travel east from Moscow, and eventually you reach the Urals — the mountains — the border between Europe and Asia. On the other side, what is there? Thousands more miles. Asia, Siberia, Mongolia…At the end you even reach Vladivostok, on the Sea of Japan — only a small boat ride from the Japanese Islands." Ivan looked at me once more. He was smiling again.

"My home," he said, "is a space between spaces…A space just like this."

"Like this?" I asked, and was whispering once again.

"Yes," he said. "A place between places; a space between spaces." I watched as the fog began to clear behind him, blowing by in thinning and thickening clouds. I watched as the fog parted way — as it opened ourselves up to the field we were in: a large field, surrounded by trees and bordered by fog; fog, in the trees; fog, in the sky; clouds near the moon and light all around. Ivan looked around him, in all directions. Off in the distance, set back by the trees, we saw fireflies — small kernels of wonder floating flames in the darkness, sending soft signals to those who will hear.

"This place, Sean …" Vanya looked at me, and with eyes wide open. "It reminds me … of *home*."

*　　*　　*　　*　　*

Allie's home doesn't look like how I remember it. The first time Allie brought me here it was cold, foggy, snowy, windy. The street looked deserted, haunted, empty and alone. Everything's changed now, and I suppose things always do. It's a perfect summer day. The tree out front is green and full of leaves. The house is bright and newly painted — the gables are no longer scarlet, but now a soft, muted, lavender blue. In the main window, I can barely make out children, running around, probably playing, and it's hard for me to even fathom: children, playing, in Allie's old house — children, playing, in Allie's old home.

I look up to the window in the top floor. She was there, once, and I wonder myself who I might mean: Allie or *her*, as Allie would call her. I wonder what that poor woman was saying to me that day, what feels like so long ago. Perhaps she knew that all this would happen. Perhaps she saw it in a dream.

A warm breeze blows out from the woods and plays through my hair and the branches in the trees. From inside, I can hear the joyful shouts of children playing. I wonder where the parents are. I wonder what they are like.

"My home," Allie had said to me, that first time she had brought me. "Or at least it used to be … once."

7

"WHAT EXACTLY IS A 'thali'?"

It's always funny when people ask me about the thalis, mainly because I do everything in my power to talk them out of getting them. Not that I dislike the thalis myself. For what it's worth, it's a pretty good deal: veggie dish, dal, dessert, salad, rice, bread and more for only eleven-fifty. Not that I tell them that; somebody orders a thali, and a little part of me dies inside.

"Honestly, there's better things on the menu." Honestly, that's true. I explain to them that every other entree is a hefty dish with enough to take home for lunch the next day. What I don't explain is how every other entree is prepared by Tony the cook, while the thalis are prepared by me and me alone.

"Thalis are just kind of little variety platters with not a whole lot of anything." Also honest; at least as honest as any other half truth goes, I suppose.

"Ohh," the woman intones, "a variety platter." She smiles brightly at her date across the way, and he half smiles back before drinking from his wine.

"We'll take two."

"Sure, no problem. Can I get you anything else at all? Yes, bread comes with the thalis ... I'm sorry? Four pieces per thali. Yeah, you should have plenty. Okay, great. I'll be right back with your papadams!"

I go to the back and start getting all the stuff out of the fridge. Kheer, raita and salad go in the round tin bowls, mixed pickle in the tiny little porcelain bowls and all the rest of it. Tony ignores me mostly, his attention on the stove top as he pours coconut milk into a simmering onion gravy.

"Uh oh," Steve says, walking up beside me. "A thali! *Two* thalis!"

"Yeah, my favorite."

Steve grins and wipes the grease from his hands on his long, flowing red gown—what an Indian would call his "kurta." His is dark red, mine navy blue. It's funny, working in kurtas. Something about going to work in pajamas makes me take everything less seriously.

"This is just the beginning," he says. "The best part comes when they want it all wrapped to go. 'The rice?' you'll ask. 'No,' they'll say. 'Everything.' The only thing better than making a thali is wrapping it."

"Twice."

"Pass me the raita," he says, and pours himself a ramekin for an upcoming biryani dish before wiping his hands clean again.

"Gotta love the kurtas," he says, and walks away.

I continue preparing the thalis before I remember the papadams. I put three of them on a plate and grab a condiment server and bring them out before heading to the waiters' station in the back of the dining room. Once there, Steve sighs in my presence, rubs his fingers along the bridge of his nose and looks out at the customers, probably wishing he were anywhere but here.

"I hate Wednesdays, man. We never get any tables."

"I'll take a Wednesday over a Saturday lunch shift any day," I say.

"Yeah man, I don't know why you put up with it. Work four hours and don't get shit to show for it."

I walk out into the dining room and check on my second table, already well into their meal. The girl ordered her food hot; the guy did too, but only to impress her. He drinks his water with a quiet desperation, and I can't help but feel sorry for the poor guy. He nods at me with a sheepish kind of nervousness when I ask him how the food is, and I nod back in sympathy. He knows, I know; we understand one another. The girl, meanwhile, chews away happily.

"So good," she says. "*So* good."

I walk back to the waiters' station, and soon Steve is back as well. He stretches out languidly and covers his mouth to hide his yawn. "What are you up to tonight?" he asks.

"Stopping by Allie's," I mutter, and lean on the stainless steel table for support.

"I hear ya. How'd the weekend go?"

" …Okay."

"Yeah?" Steve laughs. "Well, that's what you get for agreeing to go on a suicide trek for your anniversary. Not that I blame you—if I were dating Allie I'd probably go along with just about anything." Steve laughs more. "I don't know how you found her, man. Gotta hand it to ya." Steve laughs and looks to me to laugh too, and when I don't he calms himself down and tries to pass himself off, turning dramatically so that his red kurta flows like a cape.

"Where does Allie live, anyway?"

"The Orphanage."

"The Orphanage?" he says, looking up. "Now I know why she usually comes to your place."

"Yeah."

"I hate that hallway, man. You know what I mean? That *long*, narrow hallway with the stained floorboards?"

"Yeah, that's her hallway, actually."

"No kiddin'? That place is hipster central too, man. Our own little mini-Williamsburg. I only go for the parties. More parties there than a goddamn frat house."

"I've never been to a party there."

"Really?" he asks, and looks genuinely surprised. "Why not?"

"I don't know." I look down over my kurta. "Allie never invited me."

"Allie never invited you." Steve raises his eyebrows, but then only shrugs. "So what'd you get for her?" he asks, " —you know, for the anniversary?"

"Nothing, really."

"Nothing? …*Why?*"

"She said she didn't want anything. I never know what she wants, anyway."

Steve bursts out laughing. "Sean, when will you learn? Girls never know what they *want*—girls don't know what they want until you *give* it to them!" Steve laughs and hits me playfully on the shoulder. "Am I right?" he says. "Am I right." And then he walks away to leave me alone. Left back at the waiters' station, I drink water from a wine glass and listen to the restaurant's quiet murmuring, its subdued sitars playing lazily from the speakers, setting the vibe. I look out at my tables briefly, see they both have water, and drink back from my own water again. I raise the glass to my lips abruptly, the water spilling out over my chin, dripping down my kurta and staining it dark. I slam the glass down on the table, harder than I meant to—sometimes I don't know my own strength. I consider finishing up the thali preparations, perhaps only as a distraction, but in the end I only stand there, rooted at the station, thinking about Allie in the Orphanage, sitting in her room. I think about Allie in the Orphanage, alone in the long, narrow hallway. The floors are stained with beer, and the walls reverberate with sound. Girls are running by, shrieking, shrieking; men running with them too, grinning, grinning. I see Allie among them, eyeing them from near and afar, watching them close, watching them alone.

I am not invited.

*   *   *   *   *

To get to the Orphanage I have to walk down Plattekill, a winding walk that moves uphill, past old houses and long, columned porches, the road moving steadily closer and closer to the campus at the top of the rise. It is not a long walk, but the day weighs heavily upon me, my feet shuffling ahead with little more than the forced shifting of my body. Lamps light my way—I can hear them buzzing at me from above. At the top of the rise the buildings from campus are set down upon me from the hillside. If I were to keep walking straight ahead, past the campus, even, I would reach the woods—past that is the river—past the woods is my home. But that is not my way, or at least not tonight. Reaching the top of the rise, the end of Plattekill, I turn left on South Oakwood and walk down, down past the campus, down near some woods, only to find the Orphanage, set back at the end of it all. Sitting alone at the tree line, huge and sprawling, out and across the land, out and up four stories, the Orphanage is a monstrosity, housing upward of thirty people, the number always changing, the setup certainly illegal; the Orphanage has a reputation that precedes it.

God only knows the original logic behind building the Orphanage the way it is. Set back against the trees, from afar it just looks like another big, old Colonial, of which the town has many. But then you approach closer, down the long path that goes from the sidewalk, and soon you see differently, the Orphanage revealing itself in phases. Now it is one house and now it is three, now it is three and now it is four. They stunt, lean and conjoin themselves haphazardly. I think somewhere they are connected together within their labyrinthine innards, but perhaps they are not.

I stand back by the sidewalk for some time, my hands set deep in my pockets. I stand there and think of Ivan—think of the first time he heard that Allie was moving here.

"Why would she move there?" he wanted to know.

"Because you pay month-to-month, and there are no commitments."

No, there was as little rationality in Allie moving here as there is in me coming here, now. My coming here is as nonsensical as the house itself—two separate porches, four separate front doors, three rusty bike racks and a lot back behind. Walking down the path from the sidewalk, I remind myself that Allie's is the second door from the left—I made myself memorize it the first time she brought me.

I don't bother knocking. When I first asked her, Allie couldn't even pin down how many people lived in the place, much less who they all were. Not surprisingly, the door is unlocked; it creaks loudly behind my weight. Ahead of me is a steep stairwell I've thankfully never had to trek to the top of, while to the right is a common room of some kind, the walls painted pale green, and past that is the long, narrow hallway with the stained, yellowing floorboards—Allie's hallway. As I enter, everything is dark, save for a lone, industrial exit sign glowing from the ceiling—until I switch on the lights—fluorescent and flickering before stabilizing still. There are three doors that line up along the left-hand wall: one, two, and three. Allie's door is the middle one, set between the others.

The floor creaks beneath me as the door creaked before. I look down as I walk. It is smeared with mud, it stinks of beer, the floorboards are long and crooked. I hear the heels of my shoes with the gait of my walk; I hear no noises coming from the rooms. I walk down, down past the first door, down further, down until I reach the middle door in between—Allie's door. After that, what else is there for me to do?

My hand approaches to knock with an initial shyness. Do I really want to do this? Why am I so afraid? I knock anyway—quietly at first, and then loudly later. There is no response, although that is what I expected; what comes next, I never quite thought through. *Knock knock knock,* I knock away, and it's only a long while later that the neighbor down the hall tries to shut me up.

"Allie's not here," a girl says, sticking her head out at me from the furthest door down the hall. I blink stupidly at the girl and look her over, and the girl looks right back at me, examining me, perhaps the way she would an owl. The girl is blonde, with diligently straightened hair and a bronze, immaculately maintained tan. She's wearing a loose-fitting tee-shirt and gray sweat pants; has it gotten that late already?

"I'm sorry," I say, although I don't quite mean it. "Have you seen her ... around?"

The girl says nothing for a moment, but emerges a bit more from the crack in the door. She leans back against the doorjamb and bites her lip, looks up at nowhere. "Why don't you try calling her?" she asks.

"Allie doesn't have a phone."

The girl raises her eyebrows in disbelief.

"I know, I know."

The girl shakes her head, and her expression of disbelief suddenly fades away, as if she were secretly expecting it all along. "You know, in some strange way, that makes sense. It suits her."

I back away from the door. I face the girl fully now, for the first time since we spoke. "You know her then?"

The girl rolls her eyes with a smirk. "Sure," she says, and her smirk says it all.

"Right," I say, not knowing what else to. Somehow, I feel like I've been caught in the act. I wasn't counting on having any witnesses.

"How do you know her?" the girl asks, and I'd like to ask her the same thing.

"Um ... " My hands reach out toward the narrowing walls. My fingers skirt their edges, pointlessly. "I'm kind of her boyfriend," I say, but I state it as if it were a question.

"Really." The girl opens her door more and stands in the thresh-old. She looks at me with her wide, blue eyes and then looks off at nowhere again. She taps her fingers idly against the doorjamb and does not look at me until later.

"She never mentioned me before, did she?"

The girl bites her lip and then smiles with embarrassment. "You know Allie."

"Yeah. I guess I do." I stand awkwardly before her, not knowing quite where to put my hands, and before I even know it, I find my hand extended. "I'm Sean, by the way," I hear myself saying.

"Rachel," she says, and shakes the hand I apparently offered.

"So ... " My hands sway ridiculously by my side. " ... have you known Allie long?"

Rachel smirks and nods her head. She runs her hand absentmindedly through her hair and seems entirely unaware of how exposed and idiotic I feel. "I guess once I stop and think about it I have."

"You have to stop and think about it though, huh?"

"Hah!" Rachel suddenly seems more open than she did before, as if somehow my shamelessness made her feel comfortable. Maybe she's just happy to have someone to lament to, even if it is Allie's own boyfriend. "Well, she was my suitemate … two years ago, was it? Yeah, it was freshman year. Two years ago. After that she moved into a single, and … " Rachel looks off at Allie's closed door and smirks again. " — then again, I clearly don't see her much, even nowadays."

"Doesn't sound like you were ever very close to her."

Rachel bites her lip again, smiles, and shakes her head. "Why so interested?" she asks, and I don't know how to respond. I'm not sure I know why I'm so interested, myself. Maybe I'm just happy to find another person who actually knows who Allie is. It makes her more real, somehow. It validates my pain. Rachel continues to smirk, as if amused by my curiosity, something about this giving her satisfaction. But then Rachel continues, her question apparently just a teasing: "Allie … never really hung out with the rest of us. Jenna, Nicole, Lily … Allie never really hung out with any of us."

The lights flicker at us from above; they light up our skin pale and light blue.

Lily. Allie lived with Lily? It strikes me as a coincidence almost too remarkable to believe. I knew that Allie *knew* Lily — the first night we met, Allie told me that I "deserved better" than her. But I never knew that they *lived* together.

And Rachel. The name suddenly sticks in my mind. Didn't Allie mention a Rachel before, too? I bring my mind back the best I can, struggle to unearth the memories of that name — Rachel. I remember Allie, walking in the woods, leading me through the fog to her old home, her mother looking down at me through the window in a haunting. I remember Allie walking in the woods, mentioning that name — Rachel — Rachel. Why did she mention Rachel?

"You still there?"

I raise my head all at once, almost forgetting that Rachel was there.

"Yeah, sorry," I say, wondering how obvious my bewilderment is.

"It's just…" I look at Rachel, leaning against the doorjamb, looking at me, some small sparkle in her eye telling me that she relishes this. Somehow, I don't want to give her the pleasure.

"Just what?"

"Nothing," I say, shaking my head. "Never mind."

And then I go quiet. What more is there to say? Rachel nods, pauses, and gives me a compulsory half smile; my abrupt non-cooperation apparently unsettles her. I'm about to make some excuse and leave, when she speaks again.

"So how long have you two been dating, anyway?"

"A year," I say, and find myself not caring.

Rachel nods, but this time with furrowed, strained eyebrows. She crosses her arms and leans back against the opened door. "Really? …Give or take a few months, you mean?"

"One-year mark was actually just this last week."

"Really…" she says, this time to herself, and I catch her looking down at the crooked, stained floorboards.

"Why?"

"Oh…" Rachel looks up at me jerkily with distressed, distant eyes. "—nothing," she says. "Just, you know Allie." Rachel laughs, but it rings hollow, echoing emptily along the tall, narrow walls. "Just can't believe she didn't mention you, you know?"

"Yeah, well, you know Allie, right?"

"Yeah," she says, and looks down at the floorboards again. "Right."

An awkward silence sets in. Rachel is still looking down at the floorboards, and suddenly I don't even know what I'm doing here. I turn to my left—stare out at the bland indifference of Allie's shut door. What's going on, behind that closed door? Is she listening to me? Can she hear? I mull over the potentiality of it considerately, thinking perhaps that this is a punishment imposed upon me deliberately as she listens, always listens and lets me suffer. Does she still live here? Has she moved out? I look back up at Rachel, as if she would know, but her eyes are still fixed on the floorboards.

"You know, I once knew Lily."

Rachel looks up at me, but somehow not with surprise. "Oh?"

"Black, frizzy hair, right?"

Rachel nods absent-mindedly. "Right."

"Yeah, I know her," I say, but Rachel says nothing to me at all. "Or, at least I thought I did…once."

"Should I tell Allie you stopped by, Sean?" she asks, and her question catches me by surprise.

"I'm sorry, what?"

"I said, should I tell her you stopped by?" Rachel looks at me from over her crossed arms with a gaze that approaches impatience.

"No," I say, with nearly a sigh. "I guess not."

8

Outside, I am sitting on one of the Orphanage's many stoops. I don't know what it is—somehow, with thirty college students living together in one place, I would expect there to be people—somewhere, anywhere—but the view from here is quiet. Up ahead of me is the campus, and the woods are back behind—there is nothing else. Allie is on my mind, as she always is. What is the substance of a touch or a glance, and why can't I hold it in my hands? The wind whispers through the trees. I am alone out here. I am always alone.

I hold my phone to my ear, as if hypnotized; I can hear the other end ringing in a monotone drone. Olivia told me I would have to call her, only four days before. I tell myself that she must know something—believing, perhaps, that with enough repetition I'll begin to believe it myself. She *must* know something; she must know something.

The phone rings on, and staring out at the path back to the sidewalk, the phone rings for a long, long time. And so this is what things have come to—blind phone calls made to strangers in the empty hope that someone might know—something. The wind picks up harder; it blows through my hair and then leaves me behind. The phone continues to ring, until it clicks to a stop.

I try again. I don't know why I do. The phone rings. It rings on some more, and I find myself both shocked and resigned to realize I don't care—all I can do is watch the trees sway in the breeze, and my mind retreats to places far, far away from here. I retread worn, weathered paths and rehash the stilted music of old conversations; I trace back

my footsteps to days in which I might have known better — to days
in which I would never have known. In the midst of it all, the thought
of Allie arises like an apparition: she comes and goes as much as she
pleases, and does not appear to care. "I love you," she tells me, and
seems to believe it. Does she love me still?

The phone is answered on the other end.

"Hello?" I ask, but all I hear are the wind and the trees.

"Hello?"

Sound, sound, empty sound: of air washing over an empty valley,
silently, to reveal nothing, nowhere, to nobody. *Click,* I hear, and then
the sound is gone.

And then it's enough. I find myself rising to my feet without
thinking; I see myself standing tall upon the stoop. Up ahead of me,
the path leads back to the sidewalk and to the campus beyond, but I
don't move forward, I only turn around. My feet are moving; they
are taking me back the way I came.

The door to the Orphanage opens, and soon I find myself inside.
Ahead of me is the steep stairwell I've never walked to the top of;
I will not go up there tonight. My body turns right, and entering
through the threshold, I am back in the empty common room with
the walls painted pale green. The space around me moves; I am in
the hallway — the long, long, claustrophobic hallway. All of it glows.
EXIT, the red sign illuminates; it is the only light that is on. My body
moves ahead, trapped along a track, and now my hand is extended
out in front of me. It is reaching — reaching for Allie's doorknob.
There will be no knocking, this time around; my body is ready to
break down the door.

But the door opens. Standing there, watching as the door swings
seamlessly in front of me, it dawns on me that Allie never locked
it — it occurs to me that Allie never cared.

My consciousness crashes back to the physicality of my frame as I
feel the sinking drop in the pit of my stomach. I look out at the blank
abyss of Allie's unlit room and feel the sensation wash over me all
at once — prickling down the length of my spine, dripping in drops
in the sweat of my palms. My fluttered heart already knows what is
coming — it's asking me why I never listened before.

I close my eyes and measure my breaths — try to regain composure
in the dark of this room. My body floats away from this place — it dis-
lodges itself and finds blackness all around. I see myself, a mere vision

playing in my mind's eye: descending, aerially through time—to this valley, in this town, near those woods, in this orphanage, down that hallway, through the middle door, and now—here—in this room—where my winding path has led me at last.

My hands search for the light switch I know to be along the wall, and find it, soon. There is one last deep breath before the plunge and then—light, swallowing me in its immediacy. Allie's room, set there before me to see as I please.

And there is—nothing; nothing, and somehow I knew it right from the start. I hear the lone light drone from the ceiling in the way a light only can in an empty, echoing room. Allie's bed is gone. Her books are gone, her art prints; but there is dust, and that she has left for me in every last corner.

And then—something—and somehow, I'm not even surprised by what she has left: one single hardcover in the center of the room, and I know what it is before I approach.

I stand in the doorway for a long time. Over in the next room, perhaps Rachel has heard me enter. Perhaps Rachel doesn't care. I walk into the room one half step at a time. I look over every empty spot, and my eyes move over the details: vague outlines of dust from where the bed used to be; blinds hanging crookedly from the window, dirty and broken; the closet door left wide open to reveal—nothing. My eyes move over everything; they do all they can to keep from settling upon what is set for them in the middle of it all: *Heart of Darkness*.

This is what it has come to, then: another wild goose chase; another self-titillating literary game. I stand over the book grimly, look closer and see a page marked by what appears to be too large to be a bookmark. I eye the book from a distance, anger seething from my gut to my body. Allie knew I would come, then. She *knew* I would come. She could've left me anything—a note, a card, God forbid, maybe even an explanation or an answer—but no, she left me a book, knowing full well how much I hate them. The deliberateness of it all makes me sick.

Stooping to pick up the book, I find that my first impression was correct—it is marked not with a bookmark at all, but with an art print of Ophelia—dead and drowned, her eyes staring out to nowhere, soundlessly shocked that she could've drowned in a measly little stream. I toss the print aside carelessly. I don't care why Ophelia drowned, and I don't care what for. Ophelia can rot in hell.

Ophelia floats down to the dusty floor like a descending spirit, and looking back at the book, I see that the page Allie marked is near the end. I read it, almost against my will, distracted by the fact that Allie went out of her way—not to explain why she did this in the first place—but to highlight all the important bits for me with an underscore, just in case I might not understand. I read, nevertheless, and from what I can gather, there is a man and some woman—some woman who wants to know what the last words of her beloved were.

"I was on the point of crying at her 'Don't you hear them?'" the book reads. "The horror! The horror!" But then in the end, for some reason I can't quite understand, the man lies to the woman and tells her that the last words of her beloved weren't "the horror, the horror," but instead her very own name.

"I knew it—I was sure!" the woman exclaims. "She knew. She was sure." The highlighted section ended there.

Allie once told me that sometimes the things you wish you could know the most are unknowable, but you know what? It's a load of goddamn, deodorized dog shit. Maybe I didn't understand that before, but I do now. Eros and Thanatos, Apollo and Dionysus, the ascetic and the aesthetic, but it all piles up to the same cryptic, pretentious garbage. All intellectual backflips to keep Allie from facing reality. But of course Allie can't just *tell* me that she can't face reality—she has to take me out to the wilderness and read me "The Lady of Shallot." Allie, in recitation mode, her eyelids fluttering, her voice letting off to the wind. And me, trying so hard to fake it, to pretend I actually have the first inkling of understanding, have the first idea what the hell she is even trying to tell me with her poetic nonsense. A long time has passed since then. Time moves on and the world spins inward upon itself, taking me back to where I began, sitting upon a log, listening to Allie, wishing to God I understood—if only I understood. But it gets to a point when I wonder if there's anything for me to actually understand.

I look down at the art print I had tossed aside and realize that sticking to its back is a photo I hadn't noticed before. I pick it up with my free hand, still holding the book with the other, and carefully pick the photo away from the art print's backside.

The photo is of Allie, unmistakably, although just a little girl, her hair tied back in an uncaring ponytail, laughing freely with a lightness I'm not sure I've ever seen in her before. Standing tall and huge next to her with his massive arm wrapped around her shoulder is what must be her father, a knowing smile playing softly upon his lips, nearly hidden in his thick, ungainly beard. They are standing on the railway trestle in High Falls, back up against the built-up wooden barrier, the same barrier that Allie herself would take me over many years later. Who took this photo? Her mother? Was Allie capable of laughing like that, even in front of her mother?

The day Allie first brought me to High Falls the sun was setting low among the hills. I had arched myself over the trestle, staring down at the water, embracing the sense of vertigo washing over my body as I imagined the fall to the river below. Allie was so beautiful. It's so hard not to fall in love, when someone's so beautiful. After that it's all a blur. Allie led me over the wooden barrier and we were running, running, and it was hard to keep my head about me. I was in love. I just didn't want to admit it to myself at the time.

I sit back against Allie's vacant wall. My fingers run smooth against the photo. Less than a week ago, I had her—Allie—in my arms—on my bed. She told me that she loved me—that she *loved* me. "Do you love me?" she had asked, and didn't believe me when I said I did. A week ago. Not even. So many days pass recklessly, without shape, without meaning, and now only four had gone by, four that had taken everything I thought I knew about my life and thrown it straight out the window until there was nothing left for me but an empty, claustrophobic room in a God-forsaken orphanage with a riddle and a keepsake for consolation—all because I asked her to move in with me. It's because I asked her that she left me. I never should've asked her. Vanya *told* me not to ask her.

Why did I ask her?

"Hi," I hear a voice say from the door. I jerk my head to face it, forgetting I'm in a house that has other people, but then I see who it is: Olivia, standing calmly in the doorway as if she were there all along.

" …Olivia?"

"I'm surprised to see you here," she says. "I thought maybe Allie was in."

"Surprised to … what are you *doing* here?"

"I live next door."

"Next door."

"Yes."

"You live next door."

"Yes," she repeats, pointing down the hall in the opposite direction from Rachel's room, as if this were the most obvious, unremarkable thing in the world. "Just next door."

"…Are you serious?"

"Sometimes," she says, and slightly smiles.

"Have you seen Allie, then?"

"Sure." Olivia stands there patiently, and apparently considers her response to be both adequate and done.

"*When?*" I ask, and very nearly shout.

"Oh, you know…The day I sat next to you on the bus." I stare at her to continue, until she finally does. "She was here when I got back."

"Here?" I ask, unbelieving. "She was *here?*"

Olivia looks at me lightly and smiles so stupidly it makes me sick. "This *is* her room, you know."

"Yeah but…you…you didn't talk to her—did you?"

"Talk to her?" she asks, and suddenly smiles fully. "I like talking to Allie."

I blink a few times before allowing my head to arch back and lie against the wall. I sigh audibly, and don't make it a point to hide it. "Oh, what the hell," I mutter aimlessly. "What the hell."

"Where is Allie, anyway?" Olivia looks around the room non-chalantly, as if its complete emptiness meant that maybe Allie had popped out for lunch.

I look back at Olivia and can hardly believe a word that she says. "What?" I ask.

"Do you know where Allie is?"

"…Are you serious?"

"I said do you know where she is?"

"NO!"

"Really?" she asks, and she looks genuinely surprised.

"NO!"

"Really?" Olivia stands still. She looks about the room before closing her eyes. "That's strange." Olivia opens her eyes and looks right at me. "Very strange."

"Yeah? Really? Welcome to my life."

Olivia cocks her head at me, apparently amused. "How can your life be strange?"

"Well," I say, nearly laughing, "where to begin?"

"The word strange means 'from elsewhere,' 'foreign,' 'unfamiliar.'"

"…What?" Olivia looks at me, and is wearing that stupid smile again. So stupid I want to wipe it right off her face. "What … are you *talking* about?"

"I'm just saying," she says, smiling, "how can your own life be unfamiliar to you?"

"Oh, what the *fuck*!" I groan, pulling at my hair. "What the fuck is *with* you people! Do you *listen* to yourself? Why can't the word 'strange' just be what it is? What the hell is the need for every little thing to be so goddamn complicated?"

Olivia hums with interest. "And so, the word 'strange' becomes estranged from itself!" Olivia laughs in a twittering. "Language really is remarkably useless sometimes, don't you think?"

"Oh, what the hell," I mutter, lowering and shaking my head. "What the hell." Olivia, meanwhile, just stands over me in the doorway, eyeing me curiously and perhaps with an interest.

"Tell me something Olivia," I say, looking up at her. "Why is it that those who seem to think that language is the most useless are the ones who insist upon reciting it all the time?"

"Hmm?"

"They're the ones who insist on telling stories the most — who insist upon living by them. Even when they pretend to not be telling a story, they're only telling another story about the uselessness of stories themselves." Olivia continues to look at me, vacantly. "Are you listening to me?" I snap. "Is this all you people have? Are you so lost in symbols that the world itself bears no meaning?"

"You know, Sean," Olivia says pleasantly, "you're smarter than you look."

"Hah!" I bark emptily, and lay back against the wall. "I just don't understand," I say, and I'm surprised to feel myself smiling, and soon even laughing. "I'm not smart, Olivia … I'm just simple." I wait for a reply, but get none. I look up at her, but she is just staring at me, ridiculous and wide-eyed. "Sorry," I say, but Olivia looks unfazed. "I'm not like this usually. I'm really not."

"That's why I wanted you to call me."

"Yeah, well, you want to talk about strange, that's exactly what my life has become. Unfamiliar. Foreign. From elsewhere and afar. One day everything's happy-go-lucky, just hunky dory, then the next thing I know I'm having sex dreams with the Hindu god of death dancing through it, and when I wake up I'm a different person, spouting and thinking nonsense, going insane and going goddamn mad and in the process scaring off my goddamn girlfriend."

"Oh!" Olivia gasps, " — that sounds interesting."

"Oh, yeah?" I ask, looking up at her with an annoyed humoring. "Why's that?"

Olivia smiles. "Why are you trying so hard to deny your own experiences?" she asks. "You felt different afterward, didn't you?"

"I feel different now."

"You'll feel different tomorrow," she says, shrugging. "Mind moves in a flow."

"Is this why I had to call you?" I ask, getting up from the floor, gripping the book in my hand. "So you could tell me that this, too, shall pass?"

Olivia cocks her head to one side. "Is that a quote from something?"

"Forget it," I say, rolling my eyes.

"That's a nice quote. I like that quote."

"You can keep it," I say, walking past her toward the open door. "I'm leaving."

"Where are you going?" she calls after me.

"I'm going back," I say over my shoulder.

"Back where?" she asks, but I don't even cast her a glance. "Where exactly is 'back'?"

"Back to the start," I say, walking through the threshold into the hallway. "Back to where this all began."

"Sean." I stop in my tracks. Olivia's voice is loud, low, serious, and graver than I have ever heard it before. I turn slowly to face her like an old, creaking door; when I do, Olivia looks as I have seen her only one time before. Her eyes stare into my eyes like spotlights; they are shining into me with brightness, I can see.

"Why did you call me?" she asks, and her tone hasn't shifted. Her eyes — her eyes spiral into mine. I feel lost in that stare, feel naked, exposed — attracted, even. I want to move closer. I want to run away. I want to cry and dig myself a hole to die in.

"Why didn't you answer?" I banter back, weakly. Olivia, for her part, stands trained on me, her glare never leaving.

Olivia's eyes swirl into mine in a maelstrom. They growl in intensity and threaten to obliterate me completely. "Why do you want to speak to Rachel?" she says.

I stand there silently for some time, reluctant to give the real answer.

Her eyes widen and deepen their grip in my brain. *WHY DO YOU WANT TO SPEAK TO RACHEL?* I hear, louder than ever. *WHY?*

I do everything I can to break the stare. My feet shuffle in futility. I try to raise my hands, as if to shift my head manually, but find myself helpless to do so much as move.

SEAN!

"I want to get the facts," I say, and nearly murmur, " —is it really so much to ask?"

WHOSE FACTS?

"Her facts."

Olivia smiles, and her eyes fade all at once. The air settles, and soon I can hear the sound of my own breath. My eyes dart in every direction, their power to move returned. The long, narrow hallway; the soft, glowing red exit signs; the three lonely doors. And Olivia—looking as she did before. Olivia: small, mousey, waif-like…even dumb.

"Ah," Olivia says, and raises her chin, "I see." And then she leaves. Says nothing, and only walks right past me in the doorway and out down the hall.

"Where…where are you going?" I ask, and run after her before stopping short.

"I have no *facts* to give you, Sean," she says derisively, continuing to walk ahead. "Maybe I'll see you, some other time."

My brain seizes as I stand there, stuttering in the hall, watching Olivia go. My mouth opens, as if to call after her, but I only find my hand, outstretched pointlessly in the direction she has already gone. Time slows, and my body twists and looks over the vacated scene: at Allie's empty, evacuated room, with *Heart of Darkness* still sitting in the center; at Rachel's shut door at the end of the hall. The door glows red in the exit sign; it beckons me silently in call. My hand remains outstretched and I stand there, looking at Rachel's glowing, shut, red door for what feels to be a long, long time—the last few seconds I have before I know I must make a decision, and this time for once and for all.

"Olivia!" I shout, turning around, running in the direction she went. "Wait!"

9

Oɴᴄᴇ, I ᴡᴀs sʟᴇᴇᴘɪɴɢ. The woman I had been with for the last year was asleep with me, too — I was holding her close in my arms. That night I slept and dreamed dark dreams of a man I didn't recognize. Glowing, faintly luminescent, it was difficult to tell if he was a man or a woman. His skin was smooth and wreathed vermiculate with vines, his black hair long, straight, and liquid like gold. I felt him calling to me in the darkness, that night. He was dancing; dancing. I didn't know what he wanted from me. I didn't and couldn't understand. All I could do was watch him safely from a distance — watch him dance softly alone in the darkness; like distant summer lightning crying silently in the night.

The next morning I felt different than I ever had before. I asked my girlfriend, awake in my arms, whether she wanted to move in with me or not. She was scared. I had been too, up until that night. I wanted her to know that she didn't have to be — that none of us had to, and that everything was a choice, just so long as we wanted it to be. I didn't know how to say it. I didn't know how to let her know. She was frightened.

The next night she left me; the time had come for us both. After that, I felt scared again, confused. I scoured the town, looking for her, pointlessly. I wanted answers, facts, explanations, truths. I forgot the difference, between truths and the Truth — I forgot the man's dance, and all that it meant.

Why did she leave me?
It didn't matter.
How could that be?
But it didn't matter.

10

Somehow, the last place I expected Olivia to bring me was the campus, but that is exactly where we have gone. It's been three months now, since classes last ended, a lifetime ago in early May. A few short months pass, and campus changes — it becomes foreign, strange, and unfamiliar; unpopulated by the ranks of students that fill it during its semesters, campus is abandoned to retreat in its shell. Tonight the campus is open, wide, and silent, save the softness of our steps. Olivia walks ahead of me, as quiet as she has been since we left. She hasn't even said a word. I don't know why I'm here, or even why she's taken me. All I know is that now I must follow.

Olivia and I walk through what is usually called the "old" part of campus. Old Main stands neo-classically on our right, while on the left spreads out the main quad. A large field that slopes out to other buildings beyond, the quad is often filled with students: sandaled, bearded frisbee players; couples on shaded, overlooking benches, holding each other closely; women, tanning in bikinis, lying on their backs, wearing dark sunglasses, pretending not to care; and feminists — topless — sitting on picnic blankets, eyeing men who dared eye them first. That is my town; this is my campus. Tonight, however, the quad lies naked and undisturbed. Tonight, there is no one; tonight, it is empty.

Olivia continues to walk ahead. Together, we pass through the last stretch of the old campus and make it to the new. Our path has taken us to the main concourse: a wide, opened artery with academic buildings lining the path on either side. Built in the seventies, the buildings are little more than brown, concrete boxes. The faculty tower hovers above us for ten stories. I hear a vent click on. A great bellowing groan roars out from the depths of its blackness like the rasping respiration of the campus itself. Olivia continues to walk on ahead.

At the end of the concourse is the Sojourner Truth Library; Olivia leads me up wide, elongated stairs that lead us up its left side. At the top we come upon a secondary quad, surrounded on all sides by dormitory halls. Paths lead through patches of grass, and there are trees that shade the way. Olivia stands still in the silence and soon I can hear the buzzing of lampposts. Their sound calls them to attention—the whole quad is lit with their blue, pulsing light. I turn around, briefly—behind, the lamps blare yellow and orange into the vacuity of the concourse below. I can hear the vents, groaning out their unkempt yearnings in the distance; the silence is fuller than I might have supposed.

Olivia stands with her back to me, and it isn't clear to me what she's looking at. "Olivia … where are we *going*?"

Olivia turns to face me, but only slightly. "Why did you come here?" she asks, and it's the first thing she's said to me since we left. "Why are you here?"

"I called you, you know." I can see a smile play upon her lips.

"I know," she says, and turns away from me. "I know."

A lamppost flickers and then shuts off abruptly, and now Olivia is darker than before. She is silhouetted from another lamppost ahead—her messy, brown hair is glowing blue from behind. "I thought you were going to go speak with Rachel," she says. "You were going to go get some answers."

"For a moment, I thought I was going to, too … Now I'm just here with you."

"Hmm," she hums lightly, her head tilting. "With me … " Olivia's voice trails off in the darkness, and once again all I can hear are the lampposts' repetitive drone. "Come on," she says, "let's keep going."

The path cuts diagonally across the rectangular quad, parting its route through sugar maples that line our way. The lampposts lighting the whole grassy field open for all to see, the path eventually cuts between two dormitory halls and then heads back down in a descent—apparently the quad was set at the top of a hill. The path winds down narrowly with the concrete buildings on both sides, turns to the right steeply, and then opens up abruptly to a mist-skirted pond.

"Mist," Olivia says, stopping. Mist. The word carries on in the air.

My mind thinks distantly of Allie—of a word called *mystes*, told to me long, long ago. "*Mystes*," I hear Allie say, whispering in my ear. "*Mystes*," "*musterion*," and then "*mystic*," too.

The pond is man-made, is well lit and encircled by benches and lamps and by trees. Above us, the sky is overcast and moonless; but looking closely, I can see its whispered presence, hiding behind the clouds, but a milky luminescence in an otherwise sightless night. To our immediate left and right are the dorms we have just cut between to come here; and out in the distance, on the far side of the pond, I can see my old dorm from freshman year, emerging at the shore past the edges of the mist. The truth of what's happening strikes me all at once.

I stop in my path. "Olivia," I say, and Olivia stops too, just by the pond's shallow embankment. Ahead, there is a bridge that crosses the pond's narrowest part. After that, there's a crossroads: to the right, following the contours of the pond is a path that leads to my old dorm, shrouded in the thickening air; but straight ahead, just opposite the bridge's far side, are the woods—and past that, is the river—past that, is my home.

"You know I live on the other side of those woods?" I say, motioning to the beaten path that leads off from the walkway and into the trees.

"By the river," Olivia says, and I can't quite tell if she's asking or telling.

"I just realized—Allie would've walked this way." Olivia looks at me, with wide and open eyes. "When she would walk from her place to mine, I mean." I look over the panorama spread before me, and prop my hands upon my waist. "She never did take roads," I say, "even if she were going from this place to that."

"We're not going that way," she says. "You know that, don't you?"

I stand there for a long time, perhaps thinking over what Olivia has said to me, perhaps merely envisioning Allie there before me. Up till now, from the walk from the Orphanage to here, I have been retracing Allie's steps. Allie—coming in through my backdoor, straight off the rail trail and the river behind. Allie would walk this way—*Allie would walk this way.*

But we're at a crossroads, Olivia and I. And we're not going that way—back to the river, to my home. I turn to look at Olivia. She has been waiting patiently for me all this time, only so now we could leave Allie behind.

"We're going where I think we're going," I say, "aren't we?"

"Hmm," she hums. "Yes."

Olivia walks on ahead, and I follow back behind.

Olivia and I walk along the lone footbridge, over the narrowest part of the pond. Looking over on my right, I regard my old dormitory hall, sleeping at the far end, perhaps a hundred yards away. It's amazing, how long ago that first year feels to me now — long nights spent with Steve, drunk, running through this very place, our arms outstretched, grasping at nothing. So many of my memories can be gathered up and held here in this place — so few of them involve Allie, and the thought surprises me as soon as I think it. I can see her, so clearly — can picture her very walks through these paths — but she is alone — she is *always* alone. There were so few times that she was actually with me — Allie was always off, away on her own.

I take a deep breath and watch my feet as I walk. Rachel, Lily, Allie, Olivia. None of it will ever make any sense to me — I don't think I'll ever understand. And yet, I did. The night by the fire. The night, and the bear in the dark. I understood — I *know* I did. I look out at the pond and picture Allie there, walking. I'm not sure she's as mysterious as she'd have liked; I'm not sure she's half as mysterious as she might have supposed. She is only there, walking — thinking of what? Something. Something I'm sure that's at least halfway mundane. I see her, walking, walking, a symbol of something, of what, I don't really care. Everything was always symbols with Allie — everything a mystery for its own sake alone. I don't think she got it. I don't think she understood.

I turn away from the pond and look out ahead and see that Olivia has only kept walking at the same pace she has continually maintained. She walks in such a strange way — as if she were wandering, new, through a place never seen; and yet she always faces ahead, and never looks away. There is only that which is right in front of her, and there is nothing else. Olivia does not slow down for my pause upon the bridge — she is already turning at the crossroads: not into the woods but off toward my old dorm and all that lies beyond.

The hall looks haunted as we approach it. It towers up from the fog, and there are no lights from the windows to beacon out to us in the darkness. The students have left the valley; the students have all gone home. Ahead, I see Olivia leave the concrete walkway that eventually leads to the front entrance, and instead cuts off on the gravel path that winds around the dorm's perimeter—the way Ivan once took me, long, long ago.

Standing in the breadth of the last lamppost's light, it is difficult to see Olivia, who has already gone ahead along the gravel path around the back of the building. I stop for a moment, remembering Ivan, standing as he was beneath this same light. Olivia's footsteps fade to silence as she leaves me, and already, I can hear it: the woods; the trees. That first night I came here, with Vanya, I fixed my attention to the sound of the gravel beneath my feet because it was the only sound I had. Tonight will be different, I realize. Tonight, it's alive.

I look out at the darkness beyond the light's reach. The fog is thin; there will be no sparkling darkness tonight. And so I breathe deeply; I pass through the threshold, walk through the wall, and silence gives way to the sounds of the forest: the churning of crickets and cicadas in a chorus, the unknown hootings of things I can't see.

Light dims as the path strikes deeper and deeper into the woods. The sky is thick and overcast, and the leaves block out what meager light I had. Soon I see little; soon I see nothing. The gravel beneath my feet tells me I'm still on my way. I take out my cell phone. It lights pale upon the path, but it is all that I have. A frog croaks on the ground somewhere beside me—I can see my light reflect glassy in its eyes. Looking up, I see the trees lining the path, their branches gnarling out toward me in great, reaching grasps. The frog croaks again. I look down, and watch it hop off in the brush by the path. What else is out there? What are they singing for?

It is not for several minutes more that I emerge from the woods, safe on the other side. The path winds through the trees, narrowing, widening, and then all of a sudden opens up, gives way, and the land unfurls to a field. Approaching it cautiously, my cell phone raised out before me, I move in slow plodding steps before I finally see Olivia, standing at the end of the gravel, a look of vague interest in her eyes.

"I waited," she says.

"Right," I say, finally catching up to her. "Thanks." I look over at the field set there before us. Mist moors low upon the grass—mowed, tended; the moon peeps out, opaquely from the clouds. There are bright, steel bleachers to our right. Without the denseness of the fog, it looks far more mundane than I might have remembered.

"What is this place?" I ask.

"Many things."

"It looks like a soccer field."

Olivia nods, as if this were obvious, and as I think it over more, I suppose it is. "An auxiliary one," she says. "They use it sometimes when the other one's taken." Olivia looks over the field, her eyes looking out at what looks like the distance; she looks almost sad.

"Allie never came here," she says quietly. "She knew about it—she just never came."

Campus isn't town, or so Allie once informed me; she tried to convince me that the river was its heart. "I believe it," I say, breathing in the air. "I really do."

Olivia takes off her shoes—slip-on sandals that slipped right on off. "Some people look," she says, "but do not see. They hear, but don't listen. They touch, but feel…nothing." Olivia sighs, and I can hardly believe it myself. "Allie listened only to herself, and saw only symbols, wherever she looked."

The moon casts soft light on Olivia's messy hair—reflects twinkling in her warm, empathic eyes. There is no hint of derision in her words, even if it is hard for me to hear them—only the all-seeing gaze of a woman who truly cares. "I know," I whisper. "I do."

And then Olivia smiles, and it is the smile I have known all along. "I really do like Allie, you know."

I smile too. "I love her," I say, and sound almost proud. "I always have."

"That's good," Olivia says, and means it. "Now let it go."

Once, a long time ago, Allie led me through a field by the hand, telling me the names of all the wildflowers we happened to be passing by: Stars of Bethlehem; Slender Ladies' Tresses; Milkweed. But tonight, I walk with Olivia as an equal, and she says nothing, explains nothing, catalogues nothing, and we enter the field—together. Walking for some time, we stop in the middle of the open land and sit across from each other, mist passing between us in wispy little streams. Olivia's eyes are closed to the moon up above. Her hands are set down on her knees, palms down, and I can hear her breathe in the darkness—breathe. Like Allie in recitation mode, her eyelids fluttering, her voice letting off to the wind; like Allie, watching the clouds and watching them die; like Allie, tending the fire and making laws bend; and like Shiva, dancing; dancing.

"Well," I say. "What now?"

Olivia opens her eyes and looks right at me; there is a small, sly smile playing upon the edges of her lips. "What now," Olivia repeats, and seems immensely pleased. "What now …"

II

THE COOL WIND LAPS delicately at my hair as I approach the rocks from the trees, my flashlight a lone beacon in an ocean of darkness. The wind breathes out from where I can't see, groans deeply and embraces me before moving on behind me. I embrace the wind in kind, move on and through it, my feet making their way carefully along the bare, granitic rocks. The flashlight shows me the way. The flashlight leads me to the edge only to tell my feet to not move even one step further. A part of me tells me to back away a few inches and allow myself some leeway. I'm standing at the top of a cliff, I try to remind myself. I am standing at the top of a very long fall. But looking out at the empty space, looking out and seeing no moon, no stars, no light save for the one shining at my feet, I almost don't believe it. Out of sight, I reason, out of mind.

I raise the light to shine out at the darkness, seeking proof, perhaps, of my own precarious position — of the precipitous fall just beneath my feet. I want to see out to the bottom of the valley. I want to shine out with my light and see it open out irrepressibly in its inordinate expanse to me and me alone — but my light finds only darkness. The light disperses out from the bulb, shines forward in a murk and is swallowed up in the clouds — not just out beyond the cliff side, I realize, but all around me, swallowing me up in its breadth, too. I continue to shine out at the empty air. The wind threatens to suck me out into its gaping void; it wants to tear me from my illusion of safety into the reality of the drop beyond. Everywhere I turn, there is only gray, there is only darkness. My light floats about me, thin and impotent; it is low and gaseous like a ghost.

Allie is still waiting for me, back by the campfire. The idea of a campfire seems strange to me now, suddenly. All that light. Such an excess—consuming the night and sending the sparks into the concealed sky above. Allie is there for me; waiting, she told me—waiting for me for when I return. Soon she will wonder where I am. Maybe she is already.

My feet begin to turn away from the beckoning edge. I decide it's finally time, time for me to make my way back to camp, when I hear noises—off in the sightlessness—back behind me from where I came. Allie, I suppose, has gotten tired of waiting.

I turn to face the noise, shining my foggy light out at the tree line, the beam from my flashlight stark and alone in the panoramic void. The noise gets progressively louder, only now it doesn't sound like footsteps at all. I hear branches breaking beneath weight thrown heavily, without care, without reason. I hear tree trunks creaking—can soon see the tree line sway. This isn't Allie, I realize. Allie is still at the campfire, watching the flames, wondering where I am. I am alone out here, alone; me with a beast, and scarcely a light in between.

Panicked packets of information catapult and spin through my brain at a million miles per second: warning signs posted at trailheads; black-and-white sketches of great, lumbering beasts staring out at me with soulless, beady eyes. WARNING, WARNING. Internet articles blast along a synaptic superhighway, firing pulsing blasts into my spinning, sickening brain. Words and phrases bubble out within me, disconnected, dislocated and displaced: noise, bells, ringing, stature, avoid, gaze, eye contact, standing, growling, if, climb, run, frighten, play dead, grizzly, don't play dead, black, brown, stand ground, death and deathless. All the while the trees are bending, rustling, breaking. My light shines out at them, and I can see the pines move apart in the darkness. I can hear its voice now, gruff and reckless, uncaring of the shining beam of my flashlight; indeed, it is coming right for me.

But I *do* have my flashlight. I can frighten it, if I try. That's what I'm supposed to do, and even I know it as such. I'm supposed to stand tall, frighten it with my light, scream, yell, jump up and down and scare it off. The bear doesn't know that it can kill me—*I* know that it can kill me—it has to think that I can kill *it*.

But then I think of that mindless, trudging beast, out there in the darkness behind the trees, soon to emerge out upon my lookout. My back is to the cliff side—no longer imaginary, no longer an abstraction, but now only far too real. I think of the beast and can't bear the thought of its beady little eyes, looking out at me through the fog, blind and unthinking; and in the end, I don't have the courage to do only that which will save me. I have no place to run, no place to hide, only the empty hope that the night will conceal me. And so, it happens: the flashlight goes off and I plunge headlong into the darkness, deeper than ever before.

The wind lets off and settles quietly upon the rocks and swallows me in the encompassing solitude of the silence of the night. I remember the caves in High Falls, suddenly—remember how Allie led me deep to the underground lake before telling me to "be still"—before she turned off the flashlight and told me of absolute darkness only existing in caves; only this darkness is far more absolute than the caves could ever conjure.

The last branches snap and break the silence, and my ears see as my eyes never could. It is there now, standing with its paws upon the rocks, seeing through the night, seeing and seeing me. I hear a sniffing and imagine its empty head rock back and forth, taking in my scent, tasting it for more. A low growl sounds off again, and then I hear its paws pad across the lookout, hear its claws clinking softly in the wind's wake, and still, I cannot move. The light, I know, will frighten it. I have both the means and the intellect to save myself, but still, confronted with the primitive primacy of the thing itself, I cannot move at all. My back is to the open air, vulnerable and exposed to the stark night beyond; and as the beast approaches closer, ever closer, I am almost tempted to try my luck at the fall—but the fear keeps me numb, paralyzed, and fixed upon the spot I stand.

The bear moves slowly, irrevocably, and soon it is so close I can smell it, stinking of dirt and mud—of decayed, rotting leaves, and wild, unknown things. It's amazing that a thing that smells so bad could smell me so well, but that is what it does. I hear it sniffing me out, its nostrils blaring as if in my ears, and soon I not only hear it, but feel it, its nose warm upon my hands and wet upon my fingers. What is it that this thing could smell from me? What could its inchoate brain possibly be telling it? Does it think in words, in symbols, or in plain gut feeling? Does it think 'this smells like flesh, this smells like food,' or does it just feel the hunger, direct and leaping from the smell itself? I wouldn't think an animal capable of thought, but it still keeps sniffing, as if still thinking. Its sullen, mammalian brain registers secret scents, makes sense of things I'll never understand, takes it all in and mulls it all over before finally grunting at me. The fear strikes me viscerally, adrenaline pumping through my bloodstream till my mind catches fire, but all this is within, never without. On the outside, I never move, my body but inanimate flesh to be inspected helplessly. The thing grunts again, this time louder than before. I shut my eyes, as if I could see before, and try to disconnect myself from my senses and go deep within to a place where I won't feel the fear, where I won't feel the pain that's sure to strike me when it swipes at me with its bulking paws, its clinking claws. I shut my eyes and very nearly start shaking, a light tremble quivering along my limbs while tearing my nerves raw and tremulous within.

And although the fear never leaves, the pain never comes. I freeze myself for a few moments more, listen as the bear sniffs, sneezes—although not on me—and then the next thing I know, I hear its paws, not moving closer, but leaving me behind. The beast is leaving; a few seconds later, the beast is gone. I am alone again, out along the rock-ledge lookout beyond the thickness of the trees.

The adrenaline does not stop pumping but only accelerates, my body no longer shuddering but shaking uncontrollably. My knees tremble and knock and soon I can't stand, falling upon the rocks, on all fours, gripping the bareness beneath me in vain. Savage bursts of noise erupt from my mouth in spasms, alien to my throat, to my body, to my ears, and soon I am crying—not tears of sorrow or even of joy—but elemental and reptilian, the tears flowing out as I wretch out my noises, meaningless and empty in the swallowing of the night.

The wind picks up from behind me once more, rising up deep from the valleys only to meet me, solitary in the darkness, so alone that I cannot see. The wind picks up, higher, louder, whips about my ears, taking the clouds with it too, moist upon my eyelashes and slick upon my skin.

And then the clouds break, disparate and multitudinous, spiraling and spinning around me, turning in circles before leaving me behind. Dim light glows pale and blue upon the rocks, low at first, and then lighter still. Looking up above me, I can see the starlight; I can see the moon. My heart pumps loudly, pumping through my hands, pumping through my ears, my neck, my back, gathering at the base of my spine. My spine hums and pulsates; my spine moves and lies still. The ringing in my ears rises in a roaring; it pulsates on through my brain. And then I feel it again, no longer gathered but moving in an uncoiling, slithering up my spine, cool and wonderful like a current. The crown of my head buzzes, rhythmic and excited; there are crickets and bells in my ears. The light bursts open in my mind; it overpowers my senses and short-circuits my brain.

"Ohhhhhhhh," I groan out in the darkness.

"Ohhhhhhhh ... "

There are no more rocks that are left to me now, there are no more trees. There are no more mountains or moon in the sky, there are no more beasts to be crawling unseen. Alone in my darkness, there is only me; there is only I—and I never die.

EPILOGUE

LEANING AGAINST THE WOODEN railing, I stand and watch the Roundout Creek flow far beneath me. I look and watch dispassionately, and watch as a man stands upon the edge of the railing, just down the way. The man takes the time to balance himself before standing tall upon the railing and waving down below to his family. Set near against the shallow shore, the family stands out upon their back deck, stark against the red paint of their house behind them, and they wave too, even from so far away. There is something happy in all this; there is a meeting of minds.

The man jumps — not merely dropping, but propelling himself open in the air, his arms wide and embracing to take in the fall. The man falls with speed and yet appears to be floating, the fall so long and so deep that the man seems only to move smoothly through empty space, the truth deceptive until the man hits the water — until the man floats dead and buoyant beneath the passing of the bridge.

"They fall," I say, and hear the words resonate in my mind. "And falling, they are given wings."

The family is gone but the river remains. I look and watch this, too, and soon Allie is there with me. She watches the water go by with me and we both stand silently, there being no wind, there being no sound. Time passes languidly and without meaning, but soon Allie is speaking. She wants to know if this is real; she wants to know if this is true.

I don't speak at first. And I wonder if she can see it, but I am smiling, soundlessly. "It's as real as you make it."

Allie continues to stand next to me, but soon she is crying, softly, and then she is covering her eyes. "It's okay," I say, taking her in, holding her in my arms. "There's nothing wrong."

Allie cries and says she's sorry, that she's so very sorry. She doesn't know what to do sometimes, she just doesn't know what to do.

"I know," I say, holding her close. "Don't worry. I know."

Allie tells me that she loves me. She *loves* me. She wants to know if I'll love her back; if I'll help her; if I'll understand.

"I understand," I say. "I do understand."

Allie has stopped crying. Her eyes red, I wipe the tears away and kiss her lightly on the forehead. My hand runs along her cheek, and my fingers linger upon her chin. Allie tells me that she needs to leave now, but I already know that she does. Allie wants to know if I'll wait for her; she wants to know if we'll see each other again. Taking in her eyes with a quiet recognition, I see through her—past the self that thinks it sees to the I that *knows* it sees—and my smile comes naturally and with ease.

"Lovers don't finally meet somewhere. They're in each other all along."

About the Author

Alok Joddha Hernández studied Creative Writing at the State University of New York at New Paltz, in the Mid-Hudson Valley. He currently lives in Albany with his partner, Briana, and their cat, Raja.

www.ingramcontent.com/pod-product-compliance
Lightning Source LLC
Chambersburg PA
CBHW031243210726
48287CB00003B/882